BEAUTY AND THE BEAST

as it's never been told

by

CARI SILVERWOOD

Editing: Nerine Dorman
Cover Art: Thomas Dorman and Cari Silverwood

To join my mailing list and receive notice of future releases:

http://www.carisilverwood.net/about-me.html

If you'd like to discuss Wolfe or other books by Cari Silverwood with a group of other readers, you're welcome to join this group on facebook:
https://www.facebook.com/groups/864034900283067/

CONTENTS

.

ACKNOWLEDGMENTS

My great thanks to all those who read the earlier versions of Wolfe: Emma Rose and Carly ODonoghue, my stalwarts who read my books as I scribble them; my beta readers, Jody Rhoton and Nan Ziegler; and the authors who gave up their precious writing time, Scribe Scarlett, Nicolette Hugo, and Holly Roberts. I send to all of you lots and lots of hugs, kisses, and feet fondling.

I'm joking about the feet. Probably.

About Wolfe

This book is part of a dark erotic fiction series and may disturb readers who are uncomfortable with consent issues or graphic violence.

If you've processed that and are headed onward, strap yourself in and hang on tight. This story will take you to the edge of the abyss.

Disclaimer

CHAPTER 1

Wolfe

Words. Pain and words. I could hear but the meaning slipped away.

My body hurt. My head, my eyes, everywhere hurt.

For a while though, there'd been *sun*. Searing, beautiful light.

Words...

"No one can live with –"

"Bullet holes everywhere. Brain shot. Stomach, leg. Who is he?"

"A monster, I heard."

"That's a soldier tattoo."

Monster. I heard that. Knew it was true. Words. I'd not heard words for a long time. Only cries and screams and whimpers.

There'd been blood, bodies, and starvation. Darkness. Loneliness. The animal in me growled and wanted. More females. More food. More blood.

Pain and blackness oozed past, leaving trails of words.

"He should be dead."

"DNA result is back. He's American. A soldier."

"They want him flown out if he stabilizes."

"If..."

"When... He's alive. Shouldn't be, but he is. Won't see again though. Visual cortex is gone."

The dark in my eyes fluttered and rocked.

Slowly, the dark took on color.

More days of pain, blurred days. They poked my skin and cut me, wrapped my mind in fluff. There were soundless days when they made me sleep.

Until one day...I could think again.

One day, I opened my eyes and...I saw.

The first word that came from the man leaning over me was, "Fuck." The word was in English, a language I'd missed hearing.

I opened my mouth to speak and found nothing in my throat but dust, emptiness.

Even as he spoke into something in his hand, I knew I was missing parts of myself. Bad parts, good parts. When I shut my eyes, I could find some of them – a long way away, lost in the swaying, clinging fog. The fog clogged my tongue, my head, my thoughts.

Even my legs wouldn't work.

Days and days and days.

The window glowed and darkened, shone and went black, rain spotted it. Then the glass dried until the next day of rain.

Days and more days, nights too.

The smell of antiseptic tainted the air, the rattle of wheels, the clatter of dishes and pans and things. I watched my fingers jerk upon the white bedsheet.

"You'll be fine, Andy," the male nurse said as he held me in place, where I sat on the edge of the hospital bed. "You're home, you know? The USA. We'll get you up and walking. It might take a while, but we'll get you there, son."

Son? I grunted my puzzlement. Andy? Was I an Andy? I didn't think so. No, I was a Wolfe. There was another name too, but that one I'd forgotten. The men above the deep hole I'd lived in had called me Wolfe for so long the other name had drifted away.

"Move your lower leg. That's it! You're a damn miracle, Andy. Good man."

It took me months to figure how to walk. Talking was harder, even if my thinking came good. The fog was there in my head, so maybe that was to blame? I took my pills and kept trying. One day I would run and talk, and all the lost bits in my head would come back.

My first word was a great one: "Wolfe."

The doctor and nurses whooped and cheered. I didn't smile. They didn't understand that was my name even when I smacked my chest and said it.

Dumbasses. Kind dumbasses but still, dumbasses.

I was getting better and I'd figured out one of the missing bits. Females. Not that there weren't female nurses but when I watched them go past, or change my bedding, or do all the other stuff nurses did, the beast in me barely stirred and never woke.

For the best. Definitely. The fog kept it quiet.

I took my pills and I smiled the day they transferred me to a bigger, more open place. This was somewhere I could see the sun every day. I could be outside, feel my skin warm, see the bees flit past.

I could open my arms and laugh at the sun. I could help rake the pungent soil and plant flowers, and no one cared that I didn't speak well, or that once upon a time I'd killed everyone the men above had given me. Killed them, maybe done worse. My memories weren't good, but I didn't want them anyway.

I was done with that time...

I wanted the beast asleep, forever.

I was Wolfe and I was happy.

Until the day she came.

Kiara.

At first she was like a pretty bird that had landed in my garden. She was so elegant and sure of herself, even in the nurse's uniform, yet unaware of the admiration of those around her.

I was kneeling in the dirt, gardening, that first day. Her ankles fascinated me, then her stockings as they flowed up her leg, the edge of her dress, the flash of thigh as the cloth moved. The swell of her breasts, the shape of her lips when she smiled.

Nothing new for a female, yet it was for me. She was.

Slowly things changed. Sometimes the days jumped. Half a week would go before I figured out I'd lost time.

Sometimes days crept like burned offerings across my tongue, my mind. When I saw her, beautiful images jarred into being. Visions of her. Objects. Moving scenes. When she was gone, I itched to set them on paper, but the little pens and pencils fell from my fingers.

If I was the sort of man who cried, I would've. Instead I cursed, quietly, to myself.

The fog blurred my world. I was lucky to figure out one plus two. I knew about math, about history, about logic, but by the time I settled on one thing, what I'd calculated would've slipped away from me.

I could never catch the tail of those thoughts well enough to draw, couldn't command my fingers enough to focus. A shovel, sure. The difference escaped me. I guess I was just shit at art.

Leonardo da Vinci. I remembered him. He'd painted a woman. He'd have laughed at me.

So when the visions hit, I'd sit down and close my eyes and remember.

Close one eye, that is. My hurt one I could see with now. I had a patch over it. People didn't need to know. Maybe Kiara had injected me with a bunch of health and that was why I got better.

Most of my visions of her were tame – the angle of her body as she turned, the play of shadows and light on her face, the sound of her laughter, the sound of my heart when she spoke.

In one, all I could hear was her breathing. All I could see were her light brown eyes looking up at mine. That vision was the strangest. It disturbed me. Maybe because my hands would often be beside her neck, with the thumb stroking her skin.

Only, they didn't seem to be my hands. They had blood on them.

* * * * *

Kim Phuong, Bangkok, Thailand

Kim was walking along the sidewalk in front of his favorite dumpling restaurant in Bangkok when the news was delivered. A man found almost dead in the jungle some months before had been the mythical one they called Monster – the crazy one who had inhabited the missile silo for many years and fed off the carcasses thrown to him by the equally mad Johannes.

So, he'd been real, not some made-up story.

Johannes had also joked that he'd eaten some of the women while they'd been alive, but Johannes had liked to make evil jokes. True or not, it didn't matter anymore. Or not to Kim.

Over a drunken game of *makruk*, a man had admitted to shooting the monster. Then he'd seen the monster rescued.

Kim's men knew better than to report a half-researched story. They'd tracked the monster's path to hospital and then to the USA. He was alive if badly hurt, but where he'd gone in the US no one knew.

Yet.

The facts gave Kim several sleepless nights. What if Johannes had been correct? What if this monster possessed a strange form of mind control, even if it only worked on women? The now-deceased Johannes had promised him such powers.

Kim no longer wished to dabble in brain research. Johannes had been dirty and his honor the lowest of the gutter low. However, this information might be valuable to someone.

This idea gave Kim Phuong several more restless nights, while he decided who it would be best to deliver the information to. Though *he* couldn't operate in the USA, there were several countries that did and could operate there. China for one. Russia for another.

Money was better than some fruitless chase after magical powers.

Finally, after much prayer, he decided who to bargain with.

CHAPTER 2

Kiara
Good Shepherd VA Rehabilitation Village

The email came dressed as spam, just like they'd said. No doubt sent to a million other accounts so it didn't alert the wrong people. The little symbol in the top right corner made me halt and not press delete. At least, not until I double-checked. There were five possible symbols and this was definitely one of them. A multipronged star with the top prongs filled in with black.

They wanted me.

Fuck. My heart did flip flops and I bit down on the side of my hand to let the pain overwhelm my panic.

It took me some minutes to calm down.

Sure enough, a little flash drive the size of a thumbnail was stuck under a railing at the park.

Encrypted, of course.

After that it was just a matter of applying for the job at the rehab center. I was accepted, though I was never sure if that was luck, skill, or some outside influence.

The first day, I felt as if I had a sign plastered on me. They'd know – know I was some sort of spy. So laughable. Logically, who would think of a nurse as a spy?

For the best, I told myself. This was a paltry request and no one would ever find out. My parents would be safe. We'd all be happy.

I prayed I was correct. If they ever asked me to assassinate the president, I'd have a cardiac arrest.

I didn't know what the purpose of this was to be. Watch one patient and warn my handlers if or when anything changed?

It was such a strange command.

Andy Carruthers had a big file that told me enough to figure out most of his past. The rest came down from scuttlebutt and hearsay, which was usually rooted in the truth.

He was a marine who'd gone missing in Afghanistan after a firefight with some Taliban. Presumed dead, until he'd turned up thousands of miles away in Thailand, riddled with gunshot wounds. No one knew how he'd gotten there. Whatever investigations had been done to check that journey weren't showing on his medical file. He'd had bullets or bullet fragments in his brain, stomach, arm, and both legs. No one had expected him to survive, but he had. No one expected him to walk or see again, but he had.

Now he was here, a quiet, unassuming, if large, shaggy-haired man, who hated getting his hair cut. He talked with difficulty and had obvious residual brain damage. The number of pills he was prescribed was daunting and required us to watch him for five minutes, mornings and evenings, to make sure he swallowed them.

Grand mal seizures that'd resisted therapy and unstable behavior linked to PTSD – a catch-all phrase that doctors loved – had been the reason for those pills.

He swallowed them amiably.

The village had a duck pond where he liked to garden. I couldn't watch him much more than any other patient, but at lunch hour I made it my habit to go out there and eat.

Was he too a spy? Some valuable font of information from overseas espionage? Had he stolen Russian military secrets? I had a great imagination and for a few months he seemed more fascinating than the latest GRR Martin or *The Princess Bride* book I had with me. I'd observe him, the ducks, and the letters on the page in equal proportions.

Twu love. Death cannot stop true love. It was the best thing about *The Princess Bride*, even when read a hundred times over. I could read it and hear my favorite movie actors saying the words, every single time. Sometimes I'd shut my favorite book and instead I'd watch him.

"Hi, Andy." Then I'd settle on the wooden bench with my

sandwich and iced coffee.

"Hello, Kiara," he'd reply in his slow monotone. Everyone called me that. It was too detached to be called nurse by men I'd come to know so well, yet somehow from him it was more personal.

Because he was my private project, I suppose.

I'd sit, eat my lunch and watch as his big hands wrapped around the small shovel and sank the blade into the earth. Those hands would tuck the seedlings into their home as carefully as a mother putting her children to bed. If he'd kissed the plants, I'd not have been surprised.

The scent of freshly turned loam and moisture-saturated air, as he watered the garden, became a comforting part of my routine. We reassured each other. I was doing my job, nursing, watching, keeping my parents back in Russia safe; he was doing his.

Though I really didn't know what thoughts occupied him.

Every so often, he jolted me with this sharp, assessing look that made my toes curl in my regulation brown nurse shoes. *Danger* would blip up, all red and flashy, in my female sonar that registered bad men – as if I'd met him in a dark alley at night, alone, with my car keys dangling from my hand, my dress askew, and alcohol befuddling me.

My mouth would go dry, as if, *fuck*, he meant to pin me to a wall, yank down my underwear, and have his wicked way with me.

Scary yet titillating, crazy as hell, and the best imaginary fantasy ever, if only his brain wasn't barely above vegetable status.

Getting turned on bothered me. So wrong.

Except, maybe inside there, he was still him? Maybe he was locked in there, his brain churning, even if his speech center wasn't doing so well?

If that were true...

Fear would stir again, uncurling in my abdomen, reminding me that he was the subject of my observation. He was big and strong enough to do what he wanted with a woman. The other vets had convinced him to play a casual game of football once, until he'd accidentally flattened a couple of them and they'd sent him away.

Was my apprehension absurd? I had no clue. He was an enigma. No one at the center knew of my speculation about his past, or that a foreign country was *very* interested in him.

Other times, he exhibited the thousand yard stare veterans of war had made their own.

Perhaps he was thinking of evil he'd witnessed? Death, people blown apart, general carnage – it took its toll on such men. He was a soldier who'd been trained to kill. That must be the reason for my unease.

Apart from those weird, infrequent frissons nothing much happened for months. I helped with his rehabilitation – physiotherapy for his legs, exercises for the one eye that still functioned, and other things. He still spoke little, but he overcame most of those problems. His other eye, the useless one that'd been cut, he kept under an eye patch. The sunken scar on his temple above that eye filled in with tissue as did a place where some shrapnel had entered his head. His dark hair grew longer, since he growled at the hairdresser. I showed him how to tie his wavy hair back with a cord so he didn't drag it in the dirt when he leaned over.

I could barely tell where his injuries had been, if it wasn't for the thin slash that swept over his eyelids. The man healed well.

Then a new doctor arrived to oversee the wards, Dr. Leroy Hass.

I was there when he came into Andy's room. It'd been my turn to supervise the pills.

Dr. Hass was tall, lean, with crewcut gray hair that'd please a marine sergeant. He snapped out orders too – quietly, but I could hear the assertiveness.

"I see Mr. Carruthers hasn't had a change in his medications for months?"

"No, sir."

The sir was a natural with me. My father had drummed manners into all of his children, boy and girl alike. With my hand still wrapped about the first clear tub of pills, I waited.

"We need to do that. Reassess." He glanced up. "No seizures for three months. Doses high enough to make a horse fall over?"

"The blood levels of the drugs and enzymes were –"

"I know. Even so. Sit on the bed, Andy." He examined Andy thoroughly – stethoscope, ophthalmoscope, palpation of all the old wound sites as well as a visual inspection. Then he straightened and grimaced. On the mobile computer station, he reread the summarized records then shook his head.

"Andy, I'm going to have a series of new tests done. MRI, blood tests, and so on. It won't hurt, but I want to be thorough."

"Sure, doc." Andy smiled and pulled on his T-shirt.

I thought nothing of this until the doctor beckoned me to follow him outside the room. The door shut pneumatically behind us.

"Nurse, I didn't want to alarm Andy, but..." He flicked a finger at the screen. "None of this makes sense. If the MRI confirms what I saw, his injuries do not parallel those in his history. In which case, I'm having the DNA analysis repeated."

"Oh?" I frowned. We migrated to the nurses's station.

Without looking up as he scribbled a signature on some forms, he added, "The best disconcerting fact? The injured eye is almost perfect."

I blinked. I'd seen the damage, though it had been a while since then.

"I believe the man has perfect vision, despite him keeping that eye hidden."

I couldn't help raising my eyebrows this time. "What should I tell him?"

"Nothing. Yet. But I am wondering if this is the man described in his history. That man had a serious brain injury and an eye damaged beyond healing. How can this be Andy Carruthers? Only one relative verified his ID. They've never visited him since and the ID was done soon after brain surgery. It doesn't add up. I'm not even sure that man was him."

If he wasn't Andy, who was he? And which man did my handlers want me to watch?

A few days later, Dr. Hass began lowering the dose of some of Andy's drugs. We nurses discussed this course of action with trepidation among ourselves. Having a man of Andy's size collapse in seizures, or worse, a psychotic episode, wasn't our favorite scenario.

But nothing seemed to happen. Nothing obvious, apart from Andy becoming more alert, quicker on his feet, less likely to fumble or trip. The DNA test came back as verified correct. The MRI showed Andy had never had the brain injuries his records stated he'd suffered.

Dr. Leroy muttered a few swear words and I decided I should tell my handlers. Any change, they'd said. This was one.

The state couldn't declare Andy to not be Andy...without other evidence. The bulldog mascot tattoo on his back suggested marine. I had a feeling the doctor was reaching out to people higher up the chain to see if someone else had the same DNA. It was possible, if rare.

If they did, what might that precipitate? Maybe he'd be snatched away by the CIA and my job would be over? I'd like that, though I'd be sad to see him go, whoever he was. We'd begun to have small, halted conversations and made other progress.

The man liked watching birds and several species visited the garden, so I showed him, or rather reminded him, how to look them up on a computer. That led to him sketching them. We had watercolors. I showed him those too. Now the birds gained color. My god, he was such an artist. The birds came to life on the page.

A sparrow was today's focus. He sat beside me on the bench, using the pencil deftly then adding color. This was the best place to sit and draw. The bench was set back from the pond and partly shaded by trees and shrubs. When the breeze picked up, the light flitting through the swaying greenery must make the page hard to see.

"Like this one?" He handed me the book with the completed painting.

"This is amazing." I smiled. There was such pleasure in seeing art made before your eyes. Miraculous. "I don't know how you do this."

Beneath the perfectly rendered bird, he'd written in tiny, precise letters the species name and other details, including that I was next to him when he drew it. I handed back the little painting.

"Thank *you*, Kiara." He nodded then took my fingers and swiftly kissed the back of them, like some reawakened southern gentleman. "You gave me the paints, so I credit you with helping me do this."

"It was nothing. My job." I shrugged, feeling stupid to dismiss his thanks. A blush warmed my face then the tingle of remembered skin contact in my hand, where it now rested on my lap. I was intrigued by his words also. His little speech of thanks was as much a miracle as his art.

A spam email came in on my opened iPad. I stared, horrified. It signified that a new drop had arrived for me to pick up. A new thumb drive. What would it say?

Nervously, I looked sideways at Andy...or rather, at whoever it was who sat beside me. I'd not asked, ever.

"Can you tell me, please..."

"Yes?" One brow quirked upward and I couldn't help but notice the strength of that mark above his eye. Though he was tanned, the darkness of his hair contrasted severely with his skin. "What is it,

Kiara?"

My heart fluttered. This was one of those frisson moments. Caught almost tongue-tied, I stuttered then recovered, swallowed. Asking this seemed, somehow, momentous. "What is your name? Is it really Andy?"

His mouth tightened and he observed me. Was he deciding whether to lie?

"No. I told them long ago when they found me. They didn't listen. My name is Wolfe."

I inhaled sharply. *F. U. C. K.* Truth it was then. "Last or first?"

"Both? I don't know. I can't remember."

"Maybe it will come to you."

"Maybe."

He had both eyes open. Today was very much a day for truth then. Both eyes were a startling blue. Had he been concealing the healing of his eye...or the lack of injury? Wait. No. I *had* seen the opacity. His cornea had once been white and sunken. You just didn't heal like that. No one could. They hadn't even bothered lining him up for corneal surgery, having assumed the internal damage was too great. That was how bad it'd been. Yet here he was, seeing me – no doubt with great clarity, from the steadiness of his gaze.

What was he?

All the tiny hairs on my neck and arms stood up. For how long had he been fooling us? Or was it simply the lower drug dosages that had wrought this crazy miracle?

Impossible. Incredible. Alarming.

Argh. My head spun with all the ramifications and possibilities, and I rose, dusting off my lap. "I should go in."

As I walked away, he spoke again. "Don't be afraid."

I was wondering as to the meaning, perhaps avoiding letting myself know it, when he dropped in the last words.

"Of me."

Though my throat tightened, I didn't turn. I hurried along the path that led to the door...that led inside to safety.

I *was* afraid. And I didn't know why.

Wolfe. How appropriate.

I was beginning to see, no, to *feel*, why they wanted him watched.

He wasn't what he seemed to be.

* * * * *

Once unencrypted, the thumb drive said all the wrong things.
Take him to your house. Hold him there for one hour.

I assumed that was so they...whoever they would be I didn't know...could check that nobody had detected us or trailed us.

Why my house? Did they *want* me picked up by cops?

Maybe they wanted me to go back to Croatia, or to Russia? It seemed so. If I wasn't fast at leaving the USA, or hiding, I'd be in jail after removing a patient from care and giving him to strangers. I was to deliver him to another New York address after waiting that hour.

This wasn't good. I'd lose my job, my career, my country, and I'd been here most of my life. Croatia five years. Russia, two. Here? I had been born here, so that made it... I added it up again. Nineteen.

I buried my face in my hands, pressing on my eyes to stop them leaking tears. Damn them. What choice did I have? My stepfather had made one stupid mistake and now they held it over me. Do this or he, and probably my mother too, would be prosecuted. Treason wasn't a slap-over-the-knuckles offence. He hadn't mean it to be treason, just hadn't thought.

Damn them to hell.

I expected them to want me to go with them too. They wouldn't leave me to be questioned by some belated intelligence operative, whenever the CIA figured out Wolfe was somebody of importance. Having me killed seemed a possibility and it made me even more anxious. I'd probably watched too many Hollywood spy thrillers.

What had this man done? Screwed Putin's mistress?

I chewed on the inside of my lip.

What was done was done. Abandon my mother, my stepfather – who was a good man – or this.

I'd have to take my car into work tomorrow, but they didn't expect nurses to abduct patients. I could do this. Lunch hour would be a good time to do this. Some of the men were going to a meeting, after lunch, about vets and government funding. I could fudge a signature to say Andy had gone too.

Then I'd leave with him. They'd realize I'd vanished, but not connect it to him immediately, and I could text in and say that I'd taken ill suddenly. A bad excuse but it'd hold off enquiries for hours. They'd just swear at me in my absence and think about firing me.

The one big question was, would he come with me? The lowered medication meant he was brighter, thinking better, and less compliant.

My hypothesis had been correct. Inside his mind, Andy was firing on almost all four cylinders. The drugs had affected him in an idiosyncratic way. Terrible really. But...

I straightened in my chair. The second big question. What happened when his system was fully clear of drugs? He might become difficult to control.

I should get a small stockpile. What the fuck did it matter if they discovered I'd stolen drugs? The US government would shoot me, or jail me for a hundred years, if they worked out I was involved in espionage.

My heart ached. I didn't want to do this.

This was a sad day. I'd had such hopes.

CHAPTER 3

Wolfe

I was in a car. I'd been in buses before, I vaguely recalled. Field trips, visits to doctors, maybe. I remembered the trips and being wrapped in that fog. Sometimes things were so clear now that I was dizzy from the sensations.

The world whirled. I grinned at the word rhyme and at the whizz and rumble of traffic flying past this white sedan of Kiara's.

"You okay, Andy...I mean Wolfe?" A little frown formed then vanished. "Should I call you that? I mean if Andy isn't —"

"Sure." I nodded to reassure her.

"Until you remember the other name?" The light we were stopped at changed and she stepped on the gas.

"Yes."

"Okay. Wolfe."

It sounded as if saying it made her uncomfortable. Funny. It was a name associated with a predator but why would that bother her? Unless she thought of me as other than safe?

Idly, I watched the traffic, thinking, loving being able to think. I felt fresh, alive, unfettered.

Kiara had said bad men were coming for me at the village and that was why I had to go with her.

She was lying.

How did I know that?

I didn't know how I knew.

But...simply *knowing* thrilled me.

I liked her, but she deceived me for some reason I couldn't figure out. She thought I was stupid and I wasn't, or not anymore. I think I had been, so I could forgive her assumption.

Her hair was up in a bun...

Light gleamed on the tightly woven strands and sometimes sneaked around the edges to blind me. I kept looking at her anyway. Seeing her in silhouette, concentrating on driving, left me free to observe.

I should be grateful for the help she'd given me. I was. Besides, she enticed me. The uniform shaped across her ample breasts, concealing and revealing all at once – the subtle curve of upper breast and of her cleavage...the straining of buttons, the glimpse of thigh where the dress had ridden up, even the shift of muscle as she used the brake.

I imagined sliding my hand over her thigh then between her legs.

I drew a breath and reached down to retrieve the sketch pad from the floor, turned to a fresh page, and began to draw.

"What are you drawing?" She dared a sideways glance before the road compelled her attention.

My lips parted but I held back the smile. "You. I haven't tried drawing a person." *A woman.* I swear my balls tightened at the very thought of calling her a woman.

"Okay." She chuckled. "Make it good."

"I will."

"This'll take another hour before we're home. The traffic's awful."

She was lying about the bad men, but I was curious. Where was she taking me? I was done with doctors. The situation had matured. My past, dark and tumultuous, waited above and at the fringes. A tidal wave would be no less scary. I admitted that to myself. My past scared me. It was an unknown, yet in my dreams I'd seen it as bloody and filled with horrors.

Waiting for *that* to come to me was not my way. I'd seek it out and meet it head on.

Perhaps she was a part of my forgotten past? Time would tell.

I started out imagining her sitting in a field of flowers but the sketch took on a life of its own and I followed where it led, adding more details, more darkness at the edges.

By the time the car was purring closer to where Kiara said we needed to be, my hand had cramped and my arm trembled from fatigue.

What a sketch and where had my strength gone? I'd hefted boulders, once, climbed sheer walls by force of will.

Had I? Where the fuck had that come from?

"Done?"

"Huh?" She meant the drawing?

"Finished the artwork?" She turned the wheel. "Nearly there. We'll have to walk for a few minutes to get to my apartment. I don't have a parking space under the building.

"Uh-huh."

I stared at the page, flexing my fingers to try to get the blood flowing. No daisies. No flowers. The pencil had created her naked, with an ugly, rough chain circling her neck. She kneeled at the feet of someone huge, a colossus of a man seated on a throne of bones. He wasn't done but when he was, he'd have the other end of the chain wrapped in his veined fist and he'd be snarling.

I probably shouldn't show her this sketch.

That was when the color began peeling off my hand and tumbling away. I clenched my fist and more flakes filled the air. The car expanded, shrank, and colors settled into a pulsating vibrancy. I inhaled, smelling dust, fumes, gasoline, and her. She penetrated everything – female, fertile, and lush with the scent of her cunt.

Impossible. The blue of the sky filled my eyes... The reds of signs popped, the greens of the grass spiked through pavement, even the brown of the dust on the glass vibrated in my vision.

I gripped the pencil and it snapped. I teetered on the edge. I wouldn't look at her until this went away.

I was going crazy, wasn't I?

"Oops. Brandon fuckwit is here."

I dared to eye her, despite knowing her voice might be the trigger and her cunt was an apocalypse waiting to devour me. The erection in my pants throbbed.

If I couldn't get –

"Get the fuck away, bitch! My park!" The roar of a male, outside the car.

I snarled. The sound shocked me.

An orange cone was set in the middle of a space our car was aimed for. The engine idled. Behind us came the honk of a horn.

"Brandon! You can't save it!" She said in an aside to me, "He does this. Asshole. Tries to save parks while his girlfriend brings the car around."

I should laugh at that. My muscles said otherwise. Blood thrummed in my head in a hot tide. Flesh and bone screamed as I made hard fists, tighter, *tighter*. The car handle squeaked as I turned it, shoved the door wide, and exited.

Gray and rusty buildings towered above. A dog, small and terrified, poked a nose out of an enclosure. The wire jingled. Kiara's car throbbed and she glared from behind the windshield.

A man in a torn-sleeved shirt and jeans leaned on the trunk of the car at the front of the space. His fair hair rose up like a fence. Tattoos played down his arms.

"Who the fuck are you?" he sneered but stood and had backed a half step before I caught up and lifted him by his throat and threw him so he rolled along the concrete, head over heels, leaving traces of blood and shredded flesh.

"Go!" I kicked the cone aside and stood on the sidewalk watching him run.

His last word gift, a dwindling *fuck you*, made me grin.

With the car parked, the engine switched off, and the doors locked, Kiara joined me. "What the hell was that?"

I wasn't sure myself. Colors still bobbed on the periphery. When I followed her, the buildings above leaned in, as if to see what I would do next. Or maybe to bury us. I growled at them and was satisfied they'd stay away for now.

The woman's ass beckoned me onward. The darkness sifted down, filling shadows, hiding. Not so bad, I decided. Darkness was good sometimes, I could find the sun again, when I needed to. In the meantime, where was she going? There were bad men somewhere, I remembered.

She'd know who.

My shoes crunched and scraped on litter and the crumbled pieces of brick and concrete. The sides of the buildings crept closer.

"Not far to go. I don't come this way by myself." Her smile invited my assent. "You get some creeps lurking here sometimes but it's a good way to get into my apartment without most people seeing us. Today, that's a plus. We'll just wait a while and some friends will come."

Ahead, our path led under a building. There were doors in there and dim overhead lighting. Fluorescents. I recalled that name. Sound echoed.

The colors ebbed and flowed, weakened.

Again with that smile of hers and I saw sweat on the back of her slender neck, recalled the clutch and release of the steering wheel as she drove. Her fingers fidgeted at the handbag where it tapped against the side of her pale uniform. She worried.

Why?

What did she know? Why lie to me? The woman lured me.

"No one under there?" Her laugh was bright. "Why am I worried when I got you, Andy? The way you tossed Brandon..."

"I'm not Andy." The word rasped from my throat, grumbled even, ripped out through my loathing. A false name, a false past. "Not me."

"'Kay. Oopsie." She turned and backed a few steps. "Sorry. Wolfe. I'll remember."

Guess I was glowering. Her backing up sent a delicious tremor though my groin. She tripped on a stray brick and muttered *fuck* before recovering. Her eyes were big and she fumbled in her bag.

Though she looked down and spoke quietly while she searched, as if to herself, her words reached me. "God. Today is just... Why did I agree to this?" Her swallow moved that little female throat, tempting my teeth, pulling a smile from me after all. "I'll just get my keys."

Fleetingly, she met my gaze before turning to the gap in the building again, to that opening.

No one was here. Just two double-steel doors ahead to the right. Another few doors to the left. All shut. A few cars in a row, parked nose-in to the wall, and a big rectangle of light where the building was open at the other end for the cars to drive in. A cracked tile floor.

We were almost under there, in the cave of the walls. The hum of the building's machinery blocked the sound of the traffic and the sound of people. The colors flocked in, intensified, screeched a little before the screech changed to a static buzz.

"Did you lie to me...girl?" I wasn't sure she'd heard. Like, maybe, I didn't want an answer, yet. Slow answers could be so nice, extracting them.

"What? The elevator's just..." She indicated. "You be good now, won't you? This won't take —"

Then I felt something shimmy in — a connection to her, an old but new sensation. So I grabbed that link when I grabbed for her. She took a step but I caught her with two fingertips, by the collar of her dress, and hauled her back to me, wriggling.

"Hey, hey," she rasped, half-choking. She could've screamed, though. Not wanting anyone to hear, I guessed, despite the violence. Scared of being found out more than of me?

"Why'd you lie? Why?" I lifted her a few inches and shook her a little, in mid-air, then I pinned her to the corner of the building by her shoulder. "Why? What bad men?"

"I...never —" Her voice ran down. She'd figured out denial wasn't going to work on me.

"Yeah. I know. I know things, in here." I put my finger to her forehead then ran it down her skin, down the side of her face and across her cheekbone, then along her jaw and beneath.

I tipped up her chin.

"You're going to do something for me."

I could feel the connection strengthen, waver, feel a buzz of static in my ears.

Could I? Should I?

She's only another girl.

Another...like I'd had many. Had I? I couldn't keep up with myself.

Doubt sidled in and poked me.

"What?" Her husky, expectant reply pulled me back. The link was in her, hooked in, deep. She'd never get it out.

"Pull up your dress and show me your panties." I felt her thigh. Stockings. I pinched the slithery fabric then let go.

Her eyes took on a starry glaze and widened in one jump — like maybe she'd seen heaven pass by.

"Do it. Fucking do it."

I stepped away to watch. Her hands crept down her sides, as if someone else controlled them. Me. Her mouth worked, her lips said silent curses or prayers.

"Now." This was fun.

"I am. I am." She shook her head crazily but her hands still crept down. "Stop. Please."

"No." I smiled at how she struggled but obeyed.

After a strangled whimper, her fingers gathered the bottom of her uniform, to either side, and she inched the dress upward. A hint of panties showed – a tiny triangle of pretty, pink lace.

"More. Tuck your uniform behind your ass and lean on it. Then pull down the top of your panties until I can see you properly."

She'd know what to do.

At the push of her fingers, the panties rolled to the top of her thighs.

Once she'd done that and stood there quivering, waiting, I leaned in with one arm propped on the wall, and I kissed her on the mouth. I sucked the life out of her, enjoying how she let me and only made small sounds of pleasure or dismay. When I stopped, she grunted, unhappy.

"Bastard," she whispered.

Some of her still knew what was right.

Some of me did too, but I grinned. "Yes."

It was what it was. Control, complete and devastating. To her. The control pumped excitement through me. I could fuck her here and she'd let me. My cock swelled in anticipation.

She had no idea how this could be. Neither did I, though I knew I'd done this before. Sometime. Somewhere unknown. To women I'd forgotten. Did it matter? The why?

I seesawed, wondering how I could love this and fear it at the same time. The fear washed away.

I bit her neck, travelling down to her breast, livening her to the point that she twitched and groaned every time my teeth came together. More bites, downward, across her stomach to her bared and naked mound, where I took a bite and held it, deliberately feeding the sensation into her, pumping it in, filling her with the conflagration of sex and pain and a man she barely knew doing what he wanted to her, until she arched, then arched some more, and was about to come.

Mix napalm and an orgasm – that was what I had in my hands, mouth, cock, and mind, especially my mind.

Somehow I'd lost or forgotten this power.

Never again.

I let go of her with my teeth and put my hands on the front of both thighs, to keep her from sliding to the ground.

"Need me to fuck you?"

My mouth was an inch from her flesh, and my breath conquered her pussy, warming her, sifting over her labia. I could see along her wet and puffy slit. My cock, impatient thing, strained against my pants. Her only answer was a fevered, slack-mouthed stare. The evidence of my ruthless kiss shone on her lips and there were red blotches on her neck from my bites.

Her pink panties tantalized me – halfway down, halfway up.

"Take them down some more."

Trembling hands, trembling thighs, but she shoved the panties lower. A strand of wetness stretched from her lower lips to the crotch of the cloth and her little clit stood proud. I had to taste her.

I licked her mons, licked the join of thigh and body, teased her clit with swirling swipes and a suck or two. She tried to hump my mouth but I fastened her to the wall, pressing her thighs backward.

I kissed her clit.

"Stay."

She stayed, she quivered.

"Good." Went without saying, but my, my, that mindless look. Should've fucked her in the car.

When I stuck a ruthless, exploring finger up inside her, the confusion in her eyes went away. Eyes closing, she let her head go back until it thumped against the wall.

"Fffff..." was all I heard from her.

Her legs melted, relaxing. Finger in mid-cunt, I waited several, long seconds, working in and out only fractions of an inch and feeling the grip of her inner muscles on my skin. Soon, wetness dribbled down my finger to the web of my hand. Though she tried again to look at me, her eyes rolled up and her eyelids fluttered.

My mouth tweaked in amusement. She had no choice. I had her. I had her desire in my hand and my mind. The buzz in my ears grew louder, more insistent.

I should fuck her here.

I shouldn't.

I liked her, didn't I? No one did this to friends. Did I have friends?

Female, not friend. Fuckable.

"Open your legs," I ground out.

Fuckable, for sure.

I let her wriggle and grasp her predicament – impaled on my

finger, out in public and exposed, and she was going to do what I asked. While I drove my finger in and out of her heated flesh, she spread her thighs, straining the fabric of her panties.

"Tell me." I fucked her as I spoke. "Tell me why you lied. Her eyes were big. Her cunt was terribly wet. "Or I'll make you scream and come out here."

She shook her head.

"I can."

Her reply was a delicious and unintelligible grunt.

"You don't get who...what, I am." A statement not a question.

I forced in a second finger before I slurped my tongue across her clit, then sucked all of her from around it into my mouth and held the suction. Over her squeaks, I heard the elevator whining and descending.

I let go before she came. My cunt-fucking hand was messy with her juices.

What was I?

I didn't have a name for that but I knew I could control her, make this little female do my bidding. I could make her my slave and she'd like it. She'd like it so much.

"Open your mouth." I stuck my fingers in her again and hoisted her up the wall with that impaling hand, hearing her groan and suck in air, then I covered her body with mine. My fingers stayed inside her. It'd be obvious to anyone what I did even if they couldn't see any naked flesh. Besides, her panties were around her knees.

"Now kiss me." I smiled as she opened her mouth. Her tongue was in there, lurking, and I watched as the tip curled out and slipped thick and full of desire across her lips.

"That's not the tongue of a woman who doesn't want this."

"It. Is —" She began to say, so I stuck my fingers in deeper, lifting her another inch or two. That made her choke.

Light footsteps went past us, paused, then went onward, down the alley toward where our car was parked.

"Do you want this?" I whispered, close to those pretty lips. "My cock in you? Answer."

"Oh fuck. No. Not here." She gulped, squeezed her eyes shut. "Maybe. Yes. You're fucking with...my head. How?"

"Say that *yes* again."

A long pause then a tremulous, "Yes."

I kissed her, while I defiled her, dirty and languorous. Hard, rough, and I ground my mouth onto hers until the back of her head was jammed at the wall. Still she groaned under me. Then I stopped.

"Bad men? Remember? Going to tell me?"

Of course she was.

"Uh. Wha..." A sigh was followed by some delirious panting while she squirmed. "Yes. They're coming."

"When?"

"An hour."

"Good. First though..." I unzipped and pulled out my cock. It was straining to get into her and pulsed in my fist as I guided it between her legs. "Spread them wider."

She tried. "My panties."

I let her down from being a couple of feet up the wall and I snapped the sides of her panties, then I pulled down her stockings. Off with her shoes. Off with the stockings. All the while she stood there, shaking, panting. When I was done, she bit her bottom lip then set her shaking legs wide apart.

"Good."

I tucked my cock away and her face fell.

"Later." I'd make her beg.

I let her go, felt my control slide, mostly, away. It took a minute at least for her to emerge from her stunned state.

I thrummed with the need to fuck her, but I would wait.

The bad men were coming?

I'd sort that out, ask some questions, decide if she should live or die, then fuck her.

"Pull your dress down, pick up your bag." When she went to pick up her underwear too, I growled at her to leave it be.

Some of what I'd planned to do to her might be out of order, I realized.

Fucking her when dead was plain wrong.

Making her dead should be too...

The buzz in my ears turned into a roar and I leaned my back to the elevator wall and watched my latest victim with half-lidded eyes. If she tried to run, I'd catch her.

"You can't get away," I whispered, just loud enough for her to hear.

CHAPTER 4

Damian

Damian adjusted the fine focus on his binoculars to better see the pile of discarded underwear, stockings, and shoes. He was hoping they'd emerge from the elevator and fuck. "This is good."

"Wow." Guera was at his ear, using her own binoculars. "This is the best assignment we've had!"

He had to laugh. Still, they should be professional. "Remember they warned us not to let you get close? Maybe, it's true? Maybe he can get women to do things?"

"Yes and I see why. He just snapped!" She clicked finger and thumb together. "What an animal."

"You want me like that?"

Their sex life as husband and wife here in the USA had always been good. So much porn.

Her grin was infectious and he pulled her to him and kissed her. "Tonight. We shouldn't neglect our duties. When they get to her apartment, we'll do as said, watch for an hour."

"Then?"

"Then..." How to do this safely? He couldn't let Guera close. It'd been assumed Wolfe would be still quiet but the doctors had messed around with his drugs and now this...this sex-crazy man who seemed aggressive. "He can get violent. I'll go in with my pistol drawn. Quiet corridor approach, then in. If he's irrational and charges me, I'll just have to shoot."

31

Silence for a while.

"We need a taser," she mused.

"If only we had one. That could be noisy. This is supposed to be low key."

"Shooting him isn't that either."

"No." He turned to look at her.

The curtains were mostly pulled closed so the room was dim, but his eyes had adjusted. White-blond shoulder-length hair, slim in her dark pants and top, she was a catch he could never feel he deserved. Smart too. And lithe in bed. "Beautiful woman," he murmured. "You have a better idea?"

"Perhaps...wait until he's asleep, at least? We have the night vision."

It was true. Damian thought and thought some more. "He's unpredictable. I think we have to go in soon. I'm sorry."

"Me too." She grimaced. "I don't want you hurt."

"I won't be. The nurse will help me."

"No, you forget. She won't."

The stark sureness in her face sobered him. Kiara might even attack him if this man could really control her. "Okay. I will be *super* careful."

There was only so much time anyway. Take too long and the police would be here. Then...anything might happen.

They should've sent two men but most likely he and Guera were the only possible team.

"Meantime, we watch." He raised his binoculars and found the window to her apartment.

"This could be dirty," Guera whispered.

"Ohhh, yeah."

"Shhh."

Their snickering took a while to settle down.

He remembered the drone. "The drone is on the roof and watching the front?"

He heard her shift to check the laptop.

"Yes. Static but watching. The feed is still clear."

They mustn't leave it behind when done.

CHAPTER 5

Kiara

What was happening? He scared the hell out of me and yet...still, inside me I could feel a well of excitement so thick, so intense, I wondered if I'd faint if he didn't fuck me soon.

I'd never felt so *needy* there before. What the hell was with that?

Had they warned me of this? I couldn't remember. Everything was jumbled up in my head.

Hard to think.

Had he been given a yet lower dose this morning of Keppra?

Yes. Yes!

Had that brought this on? Because there was hope, if it was so. They'd lowered the other drugs, but that was days ago. Had to be the Keppra.

Or was it just that he'd left the comfort of the rehab village? Maybe that'd jarred him somehow? Please, no. I needed hope. I had my bag and inside it were his pills – I could crush those with difficulty, but put them into something. Coffee. Whiskey. Soup?

The nurse in me wanted to relate this behavior to something concrete, real, measureable. Something I could change.

Then I needed to make him drink it or eat it.

Then?

Pray.

I stared at this wild man opposite me, at the twining locks that'd escaped the cord tying the rest of his long hair at his nape. I'd done that for him – showed the poor man how to get his hair in order. This wasn't *that* man anymore. How did I get him back?

He observed me, coldly, his eyes dark and hidden behind that swaying, curling tangle. His gray cotton shirt was buttoned neatly and how strange that seemed in the circumstances. His jeans were soft denim and showed a bulge large enough to fascinate me.

I wanted that...in me – a craving I couldn't understand but wetness welled from my pussy. My desires were diametrically opposed. Fuck him or get as far away as possible from him. Mars would be good.

The elevator jolted and stopped. The doors slid apart.

He beckoned with a crooked finger and I followed. No underwear, no stockings, no shoes, and I followed without a chance of going elsewhere. The ancient linoleum had peeled away at the wall and torn through in places. This building was in bad shape and the owner was waiting for it to fall down, we all figured, so he could rebuild. I let my gaze travel from the heels of his black boots up his long legs to his broad shoulders. That masculine, almost gorilla-like way of walking was a dead giveaway for a man with too many muscles, a man who paid too much attention to his body.

Yet Wolfe, he'd never done more than garden.

I had a feeling there was a clue in that. What the Russians wanted, it must be this condition of his.

We stopped at my door and I wondered how he knew.

167

"How'd you know it was mine?" I asked, unlocking the door.

Wolfe gathered some of my hair in his hand, tickling the back of my neck, pulling my head back at a slight angle, and sending that bizarre, overwhelming desire straight down my spine.

"Fuck," I whispered, finding things had gone dark, because I'd closed my eyes.

"I can tell some things, in your head."

I mustered a reply. "You read minds as well as control people?" May as well find out what I was dealing with.

"Mm-hmm. But it's females, not people."

"Oh." Damn. That seemed...worse.

"Yes." Lines crinkled into being around his blue eyes. The man had clearly sucked up the sea and poured it into his eyes. "I control the fuckable ones, like you."

Fuckable. What a summing up of my life, of me. My last boyfriend would've disagreed.

So close, his weird effect made me grind to a halt and I stood there until Wolfe pointed inside. Did the man tap into the power grid?

He closed the door behind him.

"Go. Find some less boring clothes. Dress in..." His eyes narrowed. "Cute underwear. Wait. Wait. Before you go, strip."

Fuck.

Every time he did this, commanded, I quivered and did indeed feel fuckable. I didn't even regret my actions. I wanted, more, of him, his fingers in me, or that cock he had hidden in his pants.

I'd possibly explode into itsy bitsy pieces, if he ever truly used it.

But I undid the buttons on my dress, barely able to figure out how they worked with his dark assessment of my every move.

More and more of me was revealed as each button went bye-bye. Impatient as I was, a few of them snapped their threads and flipped away, pattering on floor and wall. Why didn't they give us a uniform with a zip? Archaic.

"Keep going."

I licked my lips, feverish. The uniform dropped to the floor. Finally, wearing only my old non-matching white bra, I stopped and waited for his next instruction. I fidgeted, shifting weight from foot to foot.

Do me, Wolfe.

Jesus H. Christ. I needed.

My pussy was going to burst...or something. Fireworks, explosions of many kinds.

"Want it more than ever?"

I nodded, frowning, distraught at the craziness of this.

Not answering that in words. He was a patient. He was wanted by Russian intelligence.

Fuck him. I had some autonomy, some thoughts of my own.

How was he *doing this* to me? How?

Wolfe chuckled. "Take off that bra."

Like a little robot, I undid the clasp and let the bra fall from my arms.

"Go to your knees."

I yo-yoed from craving him to wanting to run then he turned it on full *whatever* and I flopped to my knees.

When he went to my kitchen and I heard the faucet run, I knew what was next. At least he'd be clean...and I found I didn't care, really.

Now that...was disgusting, theoretically. I'd found the font of insanity.

"Come in here!"

On hands and knees, I journeyed to the kitchen, my tits swaying, sure that standing wasn't allowed.

The evil in his eyes when he sighted me was near palpable, but I crawled and I kneeled up when he gestured. When he unzipped and gave me a look at his cock, a thrill blossomed.

"Take it in there." He caressed my jaw and my bottom lip, until my mouth popped open. "Make your mouth wet first."

I did so, drawing up saliva, then I opened wide again. I put my mouth on the head of his cock and let him slide in, all wet as he'd instructed, until I had four inches inside, at least. His girth strained my mouth, nearly choking me, but I shut my eyes and imagined it elsewhere.

"Eyes." He tapped my nose and I looked up at him, at his smirk, with my mouth full of cock.

Just like that, logic clicked in. *Need to get out of this*, then logic swam away, leaving me high and dry, in the swamp of nothing thoughts. I squeezed together my thighs and felt the throb intensify.

"You're going to tell me all about these men who are coming."

Men? I didn't know if these were men, but I nodded, mouth full and unable to reply.

"Good. An hour, you said." I nodded again. He looked distant. "Go into your living room and wait, kneeling. I'll be there soon."

No cute underwear then?

While I sat naked in the middle of the room, before the two-seater sofa and the armchair, I heard him searching my apartment. Drawers were pulled. Doors were opened. He trod here and there. Perhaps ten minutes later, he returned carrying a small suitcase of mine, as well as my handbag. He dropped them both to the floor.

The gleam in his eyes was new and satisfied. The clock was ticking. Forty-five minutes, assuming they were watching and timing this from our arrival. They'd want him subdued and if they had too much trouble from him, what would happen to my parents?

"Got you clothes, other stuff. Things I like."

Had his speech regressed, again?

His eyes snapped to mine and his lips curled as he surveyed my posture. I didn't know where to put my hands, how to conceal those intimate parts of me no random stranger should see, and he was a stranger. Scared, I ceased to blink. Then he sniffed the air, like some primeval beast checking for the whereabouts of prey...or a mate.

I cleared my throat, of fear. "Like a drink?" I gestured at the kitchen. "Beer?" The long drive had left me thirsty and I prayed he was too.

His grunted *okay* didn't give me leave to rise and I found it impossible to do so. Ridiculous, but I sighed and crawled. This could be an advantage, I realized as I passed him. His gaze consumed every swaying part of my body. In a second, I would pass my handbag where it lay, as well as find it impossible not to display what was between my legs.

That could be a plus.

I waggled my ass spectacularly while I fished in my bag. With my hands concealed, I managed to tip out two pills, rescrew the lid, as well as find the bottle opener I kept in there. Even the easy twist tops hurt my hand.

He seemed unaware of my secrets. Well, of my drug shenanigans. Of my pussy? He could probably draw every detail.

I waggled my ass some more.

Triumphant, I held up the bottle opener as I palmed the Keppra. The rest of the journey to the kitchen and the fridge was slow but I made it back with two beers, one of them carefully doctored with the drug. If it wasn't enough, or if it absorbed too slowly...I was stuffed. Beer was probably *so* contraindicated too.

He showed no sign he detected my deceit, which meant his mind-reading powers had limits

If it killed him, I'd be sorry, and not sorry. The ache in my chest at the thought of killing him was as puzzling as it was stupid.

I'd never get another job as a nurse, anyway. My mouth turned down.

Though, stupid me for forgetting, my family would suffer.

What a shitty day this was, all in all.

And that was the underestimation of the decade.

Wolfe had deposited himself in my armchair, mostly naked. His shirt had been cast aside and he sat there like a god king – huge, muscular, and capable of rendering me silent with one stony glance.

Silent but aroused.

He swigged down most of the bottle then set it aside. "Here." He snapped his fingers and pointed at his feet, scowling as if I were a headstrong vassal who needed punishing. "Come. Sit."

Such simple words.

Regressed, absolutely. What was happening to him? Too much medication and he was semi-comatose, though he gardened well. None at all and this happened? He'd forgotten about his questions. Forgotten about the "bad guys".

I wasn't reminding him.

They'd be here in thirty-five minutes.

Rescue.

"On my lap."

He edged down his pants and freed that cock I'd already tasted. Damn. It stood up, a sapling sprouting from a giant tree of a man. I'd need a chainsaw to cut it down.

I swear my mouth watered.

For what seemed ages, he'd neglected me in that way he possessed, but now he applied his power a hundred times worse. I...lit up, nipples sticking out, clit pulsing with blood, breasts swelling and sensitive to my every motion. He leaned in as I moved to climb onto his lap and dragged me bodily onto him. Things...erect cocks went places they almost shouldn't and I squeaked in both alarm and muted pleasure. Anal wasn't some casual event. And that scepter of his jammed in me there would split me open.

I could think, even if I had to obey.

"You smell good," he drawled, audibly inhaling. "Feel good."

I could smell the potential for sex too. Raw male body, my own pheromones, plus his, all mixed up with this force of command. It dizzied me.

Then he handled me as if I were a doll, a doll with holes he could probe. I ended up with my hands on the floor and my ass in the air, my legs split and to either side of him, with my knees on the armrests. And his tongue, *there*, slurping at me.

Was I his lollipop, I wondered, sucking in air with each thrust of whatever part of him fucked me. It seemed so. A tongue and nose shouldn't bury themselves there, yet I was sure they did, had, *were* doing so again. I shuddered, overcome, and listened to him making more of those disgusting primitive sounds. I was a feast, a wet place to tongue-fuck and delve several thick fingers into. A deposit space for thumbs and I squeaked and squirmed as he again found my asshole and his thumb slipped in and fucked me, slowly. Then his second thumb stretched me, wider – my butt cheeks held far apart.

"Here. Next."

"Nooo," I protest-gasped in the softest voice, as if unsure of which bad thing I really wanted, and then I was coming in small convulsions that drew noises from me I never wanted to own up to.

"Good," he said, clearly satisfied.

Then...

Wolfe stood, rearranged my rear end, and thrust his giant cock into me. Only my pussy though, thank god, with his thumb still taking liberties with my asshole. Facedown in the rug, I suffered, and came, shuddering as he forced himself farther in.

I'd had boyfriends with large cocks but nothing like this. Not one who made me orgasm from penetrating me alone.

"Fuck, fuck, fuck." I clawed at the carpet, hoping he'd bottom out soon. Hoping he'd come...then not. Making it last would be *nice* too. I accidentally bit my arm as his thrusts shoved me forward.

"I feel your greedy little hole grabbing at me. You want more?" He laughed and shoved in another, excruciating inch, and somehow the head of his cock touching bottom deep inside me triggered the most glorious spasms.

I spaced out into a beautiful fuzz of contentment, though I was aware of him lying down behind me on the rug, cuddling me, soothing me with crooning noises while he licked the side of my face and my neck.

What. The. Fuck? Nice but so weird.

How many minutes left? Ten? Twenty? Thirty?

My only watch was clipped to my uniform. My phone was in my bag.

I eyed along the floor and spotted it a few feet away.

When his licking subsided and he lay behind me, quietly for five minutes, I figured he might be asleep.

I put my palm to the floor and began to rise...

Only to have his fist grab a big handful of the back of my hair.

"No."

"I need to go and –"

"No."

The pause was long but I wasn't courageous enough to say more. Instead I waited, propped on my elbow and aware of the stickiness between my thighs. He mightn't have any STDs but getting pregnant wasn't on my bucket list. Or being abducted, held prisoner, made to come when he wanted me to.

That part had my mind wandering back to the memory. I'd never forget this...if I survived.

Minutes oozed past.

"What happened? Wait. Don't answer. I can vaguely recall." His words were more ordered, more civilized. The drug was working? But was he more docile? The hand in my hair didn't say that, but given more time, maybe it would come true.

I needed a genie in a bottle.

"Those men, the bad men, are coming still. Fuck." He jumped to his feet and started yanking on clothes. "Get up. Get dressed. Questions can wait. Where are we? New York? You're driving us out of here."

"No shower?"

"Wipe yourself with this." He bent and took a towel from the suitcase and threw it at me.

I bit my bottom lip. A command?

The glare he shot me said do it, though it wasn't backed up by that power of his. Maybe it'd gone. Maybe the drug had done exactly what I needed it to do?

If I was careful, once outside, I could run.

I quickly slipped on the dress and underwear he gave me, then grabbed my handbag from the floor, though he found my phone and tossed it out.

"Go."

When he made me exit the apartment first, with his hand between my shoulder blades, I smiled. No power. Nothing. I could run.

We went down in the elevator like any ordinary couple and all the way I was wondering if they'd be there when the doors opened at the bottom. They weren't.

Wait, they'd said to go in via the back way so that probably meant they'd be watching the back?

When Wolfe pointed right as we exited, I shook my head. "My

car's the other way."

"I know. If your friends are here I thought they be looking for us to get the car."

"What?" Dumbstruck, I ventured a glance his way as he hustled me out the front. "You can't –"

"Shhh." Finger to his lips, suitcase dangling nonchalantly from his hand, he stopped as we reached the sidewalk, though in the shadow of an awning that shielded this entrance. There were people. People who would listen if I yelled for help. Maybe. It *was* New York.

Fascinated by his eyes on me, I nevertheless opened my mouth and tensed my vocal cords.

I could.

Wolfe put down the suitcase, as I widened my mouth. He watched me, then lowered his head. The muscles in my throat flickered. My mouth stalled. Behind my eyeballs, I felt the blossoming of...the barest hint of...his power.

"No, you can't." He smiled from under his brow. "See. I remembered, just in time. You were going to be naughty, weren't you?"

Stunned, I licked my lips and didn't bother denying it.

"Yes, I remember." He turned away and beckoned to a woman passing us, shopping bags in hand, sunglasses propped on her forehead. Her frown died, slowly, then she simply waited before Wolfe.

"Are you single? Do you have a car close by?"

It took seven tries before he got a young woman who nodded an affirmative to all his questions. The others had gone back to doing whatever they'd been doing when he dismissed them, except for two who'd refused to even stop. Normal behavior. He wasn't infallible.

This was the Stepford wives on crack.

"Good," he said to the last one, a young woman in her twenties. "Walk us to it."

That was it. She led us to her car, in a multistory parking garage. It was a perfectly polished, black, BMW SUV. She gave him the keys and some cash when he asked for that too, then walked away, her blond hair swishing on her shoulders. Her smile said nothing on this earth was bugging her on this fine day.

Crap.

"In." Wolfe walked to the driver's seat and I slid into the

passenger side.

"She'll tell the cops, once she wakes up."

The car's engine fired up like a smooth shot of whisky going down.

"You don't understand. She won't. She never will. Ever."

Scary. True or false though? I'd almost spoken, back there, until he shut me down. What would I have been able to say?

I think we went ten blocks before I summoned up some intelligence. "Where are we going?"

"A nearby place I stayed once. I need somewhere I can think. Somewhere quiet."

"Oh." That didn't tell me much.

Though what could I do with such details? Throw a note out the window and hope someone found it? Scrawl it on a bathroom stall door? Now that wasn't a bad idea.

We'd stopped at some traffic lights and he glanced across.

"Somewhere I can ask you questions too."

What? I froze.

While he drove, my mind whirled with the terrible possibilities.

"Only this time I intend to remember all the details."

Such an emotionless, if polite, tone of voice, and his words sent shivers up and down my spine.

I thought I'd had Andy back again, for a while there, then that perhaps I had the improved, but still nice, version of Wolfe – the one who did drawings and smiled and made conversation. Instead I had something new. This one smiled and made threats.

Where were my rescuers?

He put his hand on my thigh and I flinched. "Don't worry about it. Go to sleep while I drive. I'll wake you."

As if...but a sea stormed in and overtook all my spiraling thoughts as they dived into a maelstrom and drowned...

CHAPTER 6

Damian

While Guera ran out to get the car, Damian followed slowly so he could communicate with the drone. The programming would make it follow their vehicle, but finding Wolfe and Kiara would be difficult, unless they got lucky. Where had they gone? While going down in the elevator, he took a chance and swept the streets nearby. The laptop kept the signal despite the closed elevator doors – a miracle if they ever needed one.

Jackpot. He found them walking into a parking garage. The drone climbed and found the story their car was on. How had they stored a second car? Why did Kiara have one?

Then he realized the woman with them was walking away. Had it been hers? Incredible, if so.

He kept the shots of her and the registration of the car, though it drove off before Guera arrived before him in the street.

He ducked into their Ford sedan, slammed the door, checked the drone was now targeted on this vehicle and staying up in the air about a hundred meters. If it ran into anything, their best chance at finding Wolfe was shot. The programming was good but not perfect, even so, it'd been proven to work better than human command during fast pursuit in the complex environment of a city.

"Where?" Guera snapped.

"East. I'll send the drone on a sweep and see if we can get them again."

"Got the registration?" she asked as the car surged forward.

"Yes." He rattled off the description and registration.

"Send it to Arbie?"

Arbie was an agent with access to traffic records. CCTV footage of the main roads could be harvested and run through programs to check for registration numbers. If the plate were visible, if Wolfe didn't take some small road with no footage, they'd at least know the direction.

"Sure." He took out his cellphone and started the text message. Arbie could find out the details of the true owner of the SUV too. If Wolfe or Kiara didn't know her at all, that would be so strange.

"What set him off? Do you think she warned him?"

He thought a few seconds, found he was frowning. "Why would she? After coming all this way with this project... Ohhh. Of course."

"Yes. You keep forgetting she might be on his side now."

It did complicate things.

"We'll catch them. We always do."

"If the CIA doesn't find out what he is first."

"Yes." He settled into the upholstery then mirrored the laptop drone screen onto the TV screen in the dashboard. "Mind control...does anyone need this?"

"Not our job to think that," Guera interjected, before he said more.

She was right. This still felt wrong.

* * * * *

With Arbie's help, he and Guera found them leaving New York, heading south. After the messing around and going in circles inside the city, they were low on gas.

"We'll have to stop soon, an hour at most left in the tank." Guera added.

"I have a plan."

The drone was doing its job but if they stopped for too long, their car would go outside the drone's range and they'd lose control of the drone, or track of the car, and Wolfe.

"Care to elaborate?" She tilted that elegant brow of hers. After all the screwing he'd almost seen – a pity Wolfe was out of sight for most of it – it took a lot of effort to not look at her mouth and think of kissing her. Okay, he was thinking it. She had lips Michelangelo would want to paint.

He wrenched his attention back to the job. "Stop here. We get the drone down, load it with the sticky bug, and let it loose again."

"Then?"

"Pray they stay on this road while we're loading the drone. Pray they have to stop for gas too, eventually. The drone can go faster than their car. We can catch up and plant it."

She nodded. "As long as we can find them again to plant it. Then, when we get gas, we can scan for the transmission."

"Yes."

"We should've thought of this earlier."

"Yes."

The tiny battery in the surveillance bug wouldn't last forever and the bug had a short range, but it gave them a better chance. They weren't going to ram them off the road or get involved in a public shooting war. Wolfe was possibly one of the most dangerous men they'd tried to apprehend and they were on foreign soil. Softly, softly, and sneak up on him when he was off guard would still be the aim.

If they lost him, they'd find him again.

He crossed his fingers.

CHAPTER 7

Kiara

I doubt I'd slept for long, but when I woke, we were stopped at a gas station though parked away from the main refueling area.

"Stay put." Wolfe climbed out.

He ambled to a grassy picnic spot with benches and tables, though nobody seemed inclined to use them this late in the day. This wasn't the biggest highway gas station ever, or the smallest, but I was sure it'd have CCTV and that Wolfe was staying out of range.

Was it our car registration or his face he worried about, I wondered, watching him, as he watched the cars pulling in to get gas.

My hand itched to open the door and run. My rear end stayed planted on the seat. Sometimes, I'd felt his...aura weaken – I couldn't think of a better word than aura for that control he had over me. So far, I hadn't found a way out of being made to do what he said.

But, he had chinks in his armor. I bit off a ragged piece of my thumbnail then let my head sink back onto the headrest. It was just the right firmness under my head. The interior was beautiful and of understated design. Everything in a BMW seemed to work exactly *so*, as intended by its German manufacturers.

Didn't change my predicament. I sighed. I would survive this.

Even if he was the nicest man on Earth, I'd deliver him to my superiors, because I had to.

I *had* to. If I kept saying that enough times, it might make me feel better about my resolve.

My family's welfare versus that of a man I didn't know half as well as I'd thought I did?

What had happened to him in the past to make him this aggressive and able to do what he did to me and other women? More drugs? Brainwashing?

Had to be more than that.

Next time he weakened, I'd try to run. No, I *would* run. I blinked, recalling the strength in his arms. Okay. Maybe...maybe, I should wait for him to sleep too.

The drug seemed all that kept him somewhat normal and time was forever ticking down on the levels of it in his bloodstream. BID dosage – twice daily. If I could get even once-daily dosages into him, would that be enough?

I could tell him about the drug? That idea made my stomach cramp. It might be suicide to give him that information.

The kidnapper abducted... Poetic justice some might think. I was just a nurse. By now I'd be on a wanted poster, alert, whatever they called them.

Fuck.

I swore a few more times in my head and blinked back tears.

When would this end?

The stickiness remaining on my thighs and the echoes of what he'd done returned to mock me. He had me wearing an old, plain black, summer dress with a curved neckline that revealed cleavage galore, barely minus my nipples, if I had no bra. I'd found my boobs didn't suit the style and that was why it'd been sent to the back of the closet.

A whirr, a shadow passing over the dashboard, and a faint *thunk* from behind made me gasp and swivel in my seat.

A UAV drone was buzzing away, climbing skyward.

In the side mirror, I could see a black spot on the outside of the SUV that didn't quite blend in.

Well now. I was pretty sure I knew who was steering that drone. And what was stuck to the paintwork. If an opportunity came up, I should see if I could relocate that thing to somewhere under the car, maybe? Somewhere less obvious, definitely.

We had followers. I smiled, feeling light enough to float.

Some woman from one of the line of cars had parked her Winnebago next to Wolfe and was standing beside him. I knew that attitude, that posture – attentive. What was he getting her to do?

I sat up and noticed her handing something to him, money, I guessed, then a bunch of things she'd removed from her vehicle. He turned and stalked toward me while she headed for the building.

Wolfe had camping gear – two sleeping bags, plus another sack, and a backpack filled with god knows what.

"You *stole* from her?" I accused as he slipped behind the driver's wheel. I felt the need to be outraged.

His only answer was a pointed look.

"You did," I muttered. As if he hadn't stolen the BMW. This was the least bad of his actions for the day.

We drove over and filled up with gas, with Wolfe wearing a new, face-hiding baseball cap while he was outside the car. It didn't surprise me when the same woman exited the building and gave Wolfe a thumb's up. She'd paid for us.

Then, to my amazement, she came over with an icebox and put it in the trunk of our BMW.

Why plan for trips when you could take from random women? The man was smart when he needed to be, even if he was thrifty with his words. From the size of her Winnebago, she wasn't poor, and that made me feel better. Take from the rich, etcetera, etcetera.

It suddenly occurred to me that his ability might be better than winning the lottery, if you were him...

We drove for another hour before we went past a sign that stated we were headed into the Pine Barrens. I remembered hearing about this. An isolated yet huge nature reserve. Millions of square miles of poorly inhabited territory.

He wanted somewhere quiet to think...and to question me.

Crap. My toes curled and I let them dig into my shoes.

I wanted to click the heels together and go home and over the rainbow.

I wanted to be anywhere but with him, in the dark, in the middle of some god-forsaken forest that, I also recalled, was featured in a murder in *The Sopranos*.

That thing stuck to the car had better be a tracking device. If I pretended, hard, I could almost hear it ticking.

There was a rest area beside a lake and a sign that indicated camping facilities and showers. Wolfe eyed me. "We both need a shower. I'm going to let you go in. Don't do anything I wouldn't like. Come back in fifteen minutes."

Towel in hand I approached the toilet block. The showers turned out to be freezing cold but the water felt good on my body. Surely, I was getting a fever. I felt so hot around Wolfe, like he gave off some sizzling energy that leached into my muscles. I stood under the shower and contemplated drawing a *help* message over the wash basins. *Don't do anything I wouldn't like.* Those words crawled around inside me but I brushed away the memory. *Test it out.* I raised my hand to write among the water dribbling down the tiled wall and couldn't even make my shaking finger do the first stroke of the H.

Crap. I almost cried, but I washed my face again, turned off the water, and picked up the towel. I'd find a way. I would.

Fifteen minutes later, we turned onto some paltry side road made of one part dirt and one part prayer. An owl drifted past overhead, then some shadows – witches probably, given my damn luck.

* * * * *

Night fell quickly. If the sunset was pretty and purply orange, I barely noticed it for the surrounding trees, and for being more concerned with Wolfe's slowly increasing wariness. I wouldn't say feral, he wasn't that bad, but I could see the change. How many hours had it been? Five? At most. He hadn't swallowed the whole dose at my apartment.

We'd cooked sausages over the campfire, had a beer each, and were sitting on two logs that made an *L* shape before the fire, and *still* I hadn't found a way to sneak a top-up dose of Keppra into his food or drink.

If I were too obvious, he'd know. A tight pain grew in my chest. Tell him the truth – that the drug seemed to inhibit his crazier self. He might just go, *hey, yes! Give me some.* He might throw it all in that lake that glinted through the trees, when the moon deigned to come out from behind the clouds.

"Lucky it's early fall." As the coolness had swept in, I'd added yoga pants under my dress and a light sweater. He'd been so quiet and I needed words, even from him. I took the last swig from my beer and set it aside.

We probably weren't supposed to camp here, or park here, or make a campfire, but I'd let him deal with the angry park rangers.

"I've been thinking," he began, voice all gravelly – a man's voice added natural gravitas to anything he said. He could get a philosophy gig, if he spoke low and serious...and scary, like he just had.

His words had made my next breath stick in my throat, and all he was doing was thinking.

We were lost, metaphorically, in this immense forest, lit by the flickers of a campfire, only darkness around us, and here I was talking to a beast of a man who might do anything if I didn't get more drug into him.

I swallowed my unease. "What have you been thinking?"

He brought his gaze down from the stars and looked at me. His hands were clasped in his lap, though I noticed them tensing then relaxing. Maybe he was nervous too? "A lot."

"Really?" Flippant, but I figured lightness was my only defense. Make this seem normal and I might get him to lower his guard.

"Are you mostly innocent, Kiara? Or are you to blame?"

For what? I shrank back.

Something rustled in the bushes over to the right. The remains of a crumbled building lay forty or so yards away in that direction. Was it a beaver? A bear? A bear trundling in might be preferable to his questions.

"I feel like I've woken from a dream or a bad fairy tale." He opened his hands. "I don't know who to trust or where to go."

"Sleeping Beauty?" I chuckled. I understood, though. This was a bit sleeping beauty, except he was no Disney princess.

"Who am I? Who are you? Why did you take me from the village?"

I wanted that beer bottle back in my hands, so I had something to clutch. "I don't know everything. Pick one."

I heard him inhale.

"Who are these bad guys?"

"That wasn't one of the –"

"Just answer."

I tried not to say – I was ashamed, scared, afraid for my family if I failed – but the answer popped into my throat and spilled.

"Russian intelligence."

"Fuck. The GRU?"

First swear word I'd heard from him in ages. I knew the abbreviation but couldn't help him.

"I don't know. I was contacted, when I went to leave Russia to come here, but not told which branch they were. They threatened my family – if I disobeyed, things would happen in Russia."

"Okay. Next one. Why?"

"Why do they want you? They never said, but I can guess."

He kept watching me and I knew he'd make me say it, but I'd stalled. Saying the next bit out loud seemed odd, wrong, humiliating.

"Guess then."

"This." I grimaced. "You being able to do mind games. Stuff like that. Months ago, I wondered what you'd done to attract attention. I thought it must be to do with your military service, but now I'm not even sure if you're a soldier. Are you?"

"I don't know."

"Why aren't you more worried about this? Most people with a foreign country's spies chasing them would be worried."

And here I'd flipped things and was interrogating him. His eyes narrowed in realization and he gestured to me.

"Come here."

"Why?"

Though I twisted my mouth, I'd been standing even as I'd said *why*. I walked over to wait before him. My heart thudded in my ears and I watched him raise his hands, then he rested those big hands on my hips. The contact jarred me with the most delicious sensation. When he pulled me to him, I barely dragged my feet.

"I can feel how terrified you are."

Well, I was...and I wasn't. That effect of his screwed with my perceptions. I was no longer certain which was my real emotion and which was not.

Sitting on his lap, with his arms around me and his mouth on my neck or in my hair...I wriggled into a better position and let out a sigh...it was heaven, with just a smidgen of hell.

CHAPTER 8

Wolfe

I stared past her at the fire and the embers floating into the night. The crackling of wood burning, the scent of smoke, and this soft, sexy woman in my arms, it rendered me speechless again.

Words came easier than before, but not as easily as thoughts.

Kiara was right. I was the man version of that sleeping girl in the forest, waking after losing years of his past. Or was I Rumpelstiltskin? Now he was some Russian fairytale. I didn't even know how long I'd been in the US, or how I'd gotten overseas, or why I was there.

That worried me more than having Russian spies chasing me. I had a rock-solid confidence that I could deal with them. My fuzzy past was different. I needed it back but there were vague memories of terrible things, of blood and killing. Was I capable of murder? Maybe the Russians wanted me for killing people and not because of what I could do with women?

This ability had settled into my hands like a weapon I'd trained to use, for years. Locked, loaded, fire away.

I could tell, mostly, which women I could deal with. A few I couldn't, not many, and sometimes it seemed that was more a result of a temporary malfunction.

I wanted my lost past. What if someone had decided to drug the hell out of me rather than let me loose on society? That made sense. Except this power was something any military would give its left nut for. They'd never leave me rotting in a drugged haze in a low-security rehab village.

"Tell me all the facts you know, Kiara."

"About Andy Carruthers? He was lost in Afghanistan in 2012 but you said you aren't him."

"Yes. What about me, though?"

"Only that you were shot in Thailand less than a year ago. Doctor Hass believes you may not be that man even, because the injuries seen then, well, you don't have them."

"And you think that too?" When she didn't answer, I jostled her.

"I think...maybe you're him, but you healed."

Which isn't normal. No wonder she was sounding unsure.

"So you think I'm some supernatural being?" I really wanted to know this one.

She lowered her head. "Maybe. But...I think you're probably just a man who has changed somehow. I don't know why or how. Nothing in your records suggested anything unusual. Wait. No. Your sight came back early on. That was miracle one. You've always healed better than a normal person."

And the other things made me not normal. Not just this...ability, but what I felt, things I felt in my gut, that made me crave what anyone would call sinful.

I'd fucked her at her apartment, even if my memory of it was mostly gone. Maybe I'd hurt her in ways no man should hurt a woman, and yet...I looked inward, feeling the flare of lust in my groin. The thought of making her squeal in pain while she came, it'd turned me on, instantly.

Impossible not to get an erection with her on my lap.

I needed to keep a close rein on myself until I sorted myself out. Had she betrayed me? Sure. She had reasons for it that made sense. Didn't make me like it, though.

The firelight limned her hair in a halo of orange. I put my hand to her nape and stroked her there, feeling her shiver, knowing she was already aroused.

A dark shape on her neck had me curious so I pushed her head forward while holding her hair out of the way. Reflections bathed her neck.

"You have a mark here," I said, tracing it.

"Ouch!"

"It's deep enough to have bled in some places."

"I think it's where you licked me."

Jesus. How rough had I been? Seriously, what the fuck, and...I wondered what her neck had tasted like.

Bouncing from caring about her to grim, dark, and macabre bemused me, amused me, made me curious about my own mind.

Why had I lost memories when I fucked her? Forgetting the best parts was cruel.

I let her go and she raised her head.

"Anything else I need to know like...how many of these bad guys were after me?"

"I don't know. I contact my handler by a thumb drive left in prearranged places and, sometimes, if an emergency, email. Here? I can't. I was to hand you over after an hour of surveillance at my apartment."

"We seem to have lost them."

"Mmm."

That noncommittal reply bothered me. "Have you seen them since?"

"No."

Truth.

"Okay." I squeezed her shoulder. "We should sleep. You can share the sleeping bags with me. It'll be warmer and we can zip them together. At the pause in her breathing, I smiled. "I'm not going to fuck you."

Only because I didn't trust myself.

The slender line of her neck made me dream of biting her, clawing at her, stripping her to nothing but female.

I swallowed. Trust thyself first.

Then fuck her?

My morals were getting damn shaky.

And she'd been going to hand me over to people who might kill me, for all she knew.

That seemed justification for revenge fucking.

No. That sucked. Morals, man, morals.

No fucking her.

"Just, be good. Tomorrow, I think I know where to go. I have a friend who kept a cabin up in Minnesota. It's been there forever. Anyways, sleep time. Up."

At my urging, she stood then turned to face me. "Why... Why

don't you just let me go? You don't need me."

"I don't?" I raised my eyebrows. "I have no idea who or what I need."

When the light was behind her, those yoga pants and the thin skirt of her dress hid nothing of her shape. Though daylight would be better... Hunger stirred.

I met her gaze. "I can't let you go. You might run to anyone."

She pouted. "You can trust me. You can make me not tell."

Yes, but my power seemed to wax and wane. I rose and stared, waiting for her to lower her gaze, she didn't. There was more to Kiara than one would think. Nurse, spy, kidnapper, what else?

Fuck toy? To be honest, I didn't really want to let her go.

* * * * *

Zipped up in the sleeping bag with her, I managed to go to sleep. Only to be awakened in the night by Kiara climbing out. The zip was mostly undone and she stood, silhouetted by thin starlight. I lunged but missed snagging her ankle. Despite her gasp of shock at the glancing touch of my fingertips, she began running.

Leaving me? Hell no.

The speed of her flight slowed when she reached the edges of our camping area, where shrubs grew more densely, and I heard the crunch of leaves and twigs beneath her feet.

My spine cracked as I stretched. Then I leisurely followed her erratic, noisy path.

She didn't know how well I could see in the dark. The lake was in that direction. If I let her keep going, she'd find the shore where the edges might collapse at her weight. Rescuing her from the cold, weedy depths at one or two in the morning? No.

My passage through the trees was faster but not perfect. I glowered when some roots managed to tangle my bare foot and snarled at the scrape of a rock on my heel. This attempt of hers was futile. Stupid female.

I glimpsed the moon. My blood pulse thudded louder.

Pieces of moon peeled and fell away into the forest, gathering into a scattered horde of pale and dark with the rising shards of fractured trees. I sucked harsh breaths and scored my nails across my bared thighs, trying to wake myself from this miasma of wrongness. I knew what followed.

Light flared on the fungus growing on bark. Red outlined the running girl ahead. The brickwork she placed her hand on wavered then steadied.

Some calmness returned, but I recognized the signs – same as in her car. The prospect of catching her and punishing her gave me chills, good ones. She ran – she suffered the consequences.

I shook my head, flailing my shoulders with my unbound hair, whipping sense into my head.

The buzz subsided, my environment settled. No more floating fucking trees.

"I'm coming after you, woman." When she darted sideways, I grinned. She hoped to mess up my aim.

"I can see you. Nightmares can see in the dark." I chuckled.

Weaving through the trunks, with the pale-as-sin sand underfoot and the trees lined up like the bars of a cage, I had time to savor this.

The lake was close and she must've realized, because again she altered her path, dodging back through the forest at an angle – coming my way but to the right. I slowed and took care to make less noise. Thorns still whipped across my bare lower legs. I ignored them.

My senses drew a picture of Kiara, a delicious one.

Perspiration, and growing panic – in her fitful breaths and the pinched-off whimpers when she stepped on something sharp. Barefoot like me, but she couldn't see half as well.

A wall loomed from the trees. Magic. We'd come in a part circle. Just what I wanted and where.

"Stop!" I roared.

She halted, caught in mid-step, then her foot lowered. But she didn't turn to see me approach.

Simple and effective. This was all I'd needed to do but I'd wanted to see her run.

The forest debris snapped under my weight. I swept aside an overhanging branch and went to her, trying not to let the scent of her sweat and the sting of scratches on my legs stir me.

Pain, her smell, her body heat, and a woman gasping from running, almost to the point of choking. I towered over her from behind, an inch away, only touching her fleetingly. I let her feel my presence. Her fertile scent filled my nostrils. My dick, already hard, engorged some more.

"You weren't good."

"I –"

"You weren't." Looking down her body, I could see her chest rise and fall, and the trembling, oh the fucking trembling...

Fear. As well as a rising need for me. I could eat that up, suck it in like life juice.

I circled her with my arms, found each of her breasts and gripped them, hard, until she whined. "You've been *very* bad." Then I squeezed a little harder and lifted her backward, pulling her into my body.

The pain made her wriggle and drum her heels on my legs.

I chuckled. "Hate that?"

"Yes!"

With my mouth by her ear, I asked again. "Like it too?"

Her "Maybe" sounded quietly dismayed.

I laughed. I'd known it. In her mind, I could feel her getting wet between her legs.

"Shut your eyes. Don't open them unless I say to."

I lowered her then worked a hand down the front of her tights, slipped it into her panties and found the slickness. My nostrils flared as I explored the groove between her lips and a richer eddy of her scent reached me. I reached her entrance and pushed into her, slowly. When my finger was in to the second knuckle, I stopped, feeling her pulse and grip me.

I kissed her ear and her eyelids flickered.

"I'll be back. Stay."

I extracted my finger, pleased at her almost inaudible moan.

She whimpered as I stepped away, and I smiled. My control was solid. She'd not move and I had items to collect.

The rope from the backpack. Used for a tent, but I had other uses in mind. The struts from the kite the woman had left in the BMW's trunk. The bag of tent pegs. More things. I'd look and see what suited the task. Even the trees I passed gave me evil ideas. Excitement enlivened me to the point of making my dick hurt.

Her running had given me just the right excuse.

I'd said I wouldn't fuck her. I should've held my tongue.

CHAPTER 9

Kiara

When Wolfe returned, he clinked and the knowledge he had brought something metal sent my brain scurrying through possibilities. I didn't like the unknown. I had to raise my feet to let him pull down my tights and panties. My dress was dragged over my head, my bra undone and removed until I was naked, shivering, and dreading what might come next.

Silence, all had been done in silence. He lifted me, wordless, and carried me, cradled in his arms, a few yards backward before I felt him turn, walk a short distance, and duck. We must be inside the tumbled-down building.

I wriggled, wishing I had the willpower and courage to spill from his arms and run again.

Nothing I could do, except listen to the crack and crackle of grass and dry leaves, to the beat of his heart beside my ear, and to the *thud, thud* of my own heart. It seemed about to break free from my chest. When he went to set me on my feet, I found I'd clutched his shirt; a small button pressed into my fist.

"Let go and spread your legs."

Fuck.

I clenched my hand for a second, then released his shirt, opened my legs. He deposited me, standing up, on something like concrete or brick. Cold penetrated my bare feet. The inside of one foot rested at the edge of whatever I stood on, so I shifted it away.

"Don't move or you'll fall. This is a block of concrete. It's old and crumbling."

From the direction of his voice – directly ahead – I was a couple of feet above the ground. My stomach clenched. Why was I here?

I'd run without shoes – there'd been no time for finesse and I was sure my feet bled. I'd been desperate, until he told me to stop.

Obeying him when he yelled *stop* had been automatic, maddening, yet strangely calming. I'd still wanted to flee though every muscle in my body had responded to him and not to me.

He'd played with my body until I almost cried then he'd left me alone while he went away to find something...left me alone, in the dark, and I couldn't open my eyes.

With every step he took that led him away, the noises around me had seemed to intensify. I became more terrified of what those noises might mean than of him. If I couldn't see, I couldn't defend myself.

I could only wait, anticipating some random attack from a crazed serial killer cross bear cross night-walking zombie.

My relief when I heard him returning was crazily ironic.

Now, here I stood, stripped naked and teetering on the edge of some ancient block of concrete. My feet hurt and grit stirred under them when I shifted. Cold leeched into my soles; the scratches stung.

His finger pressed into my navel and stayed there. I shuddered, stiffening, as sensation trickled from his skin to mine, then deeper – wisps of desire that teased my breasts, my lips, my mind, then drifted below, to where I held my thighs spread.

I hated that he could arouse me so easily. One touch, one growled word, one application of his hand in just the right way. If he didn't frighten me, what a lover he would be. If he cared for me.

And there it was – sadly, I ached to have Wolfe defile me.

"Why?" I ventured. Then I said, shakily, in my best and nicest tone. "I won't run again."

"No. You won't. I forbid it."

"Good." I nodded. My eyes were still shut, but I could hope. "Then...I can get down?"

"You stay. This was a saw mill. You stand over the blade. The teeth are rusted and big. Fat triangles. Like this."

Metal scraped coldly and dispassionately up my inner thigh until it bumped at my most intimate place. He slid it between my legs, that sharp metal, and it reached my entrance.

"Found your pretty hole."

I quivered, sucked in air.

Such dirty words. My clit had liked them. It swelled and stood up, proud. My pussy lips parted, and I had to make myself be still and not squirm.

"*This* can go inside you. It'd cut because it's a knife. So would the rusty saw teeth. You want to keep still. Or else...bad things happen to you...to your cunt. Get that?"

I gritted my teeth, nodding even as his blade nudged into me, slipping in as if it meant nothing. He toyed there, rotating it, this way, that way.

"I could fuck you with this. You're wet enough to let it go in deeper. Maybe, if I was careful, it wouldn't cut you."

I shuddered, afraid, yet feeling my pussy tighten then release. "I said I wouldn't fuck you though."

With a knife. God.

A knife.

I was still drifting on the promise of that threat when something swished past, overhead, then whipped back down. It sang past my head.

"Put your hands out where I can tie them."

Oh, this was evil. He could hold me, control me, but tying my hands seemed a whole other universe. From behind the blackness in my eyes, I wondered why that was so.

I raised my arms from my sides and held them out front, with my wrists together. He grabbed them, wrapped stiff rope about them, knotted it quietly and efficiently, then hauled on the rope until my arms stretched above my head.

Though flat on my feet, I felt this need to balance – it pulled and made me want to close my legs. I mustn't do that. So I waited with the rope creaking and rasping on whatever it was cast over.

"So beautiful, like this. My offering."

He covered my right breast with his hand and I realized my nipples were like little rocks, sticking out. When he began to squeeze, I let out a shivery moan.

I bit my lower lip, striving not to moan again. Whatever he did, I liked it. Inevitable. Nasty, bad, but true.

"I think I promised not to fuck, only if you stayed good."

"I hate you," I whispered.

His laugh malevolent. "No. You don't. You hate what I can make you feel, or make you do."

"Fuck you. Fuck you to hell and back."

"I heard you. Now shush. No more words."

My throat and mind became bare of language. Just like that – with only a ringing sound in my ears that subsided. And his hands worked at something below. The metal blade left me then a minute later it returned and he wedged the tip inside me, slowly. Only a fraction of an inch but that was enough.

My inhalation was sharp. Deviant man.

Where the metal entered me, his fingertip circled.

"Yes," he murmured. When I looked down, he bestowed a shocking kiss upon my clit. I made a strangled noise.

"Speak," he said.

"Don't."

Wolfe laughed.

Already my thighs ached from having to stand as I was – with my legs apart and unmoving.

"Is it hard to keep still? Poor girl. This is tied to the end of a stick. The stick is wedged next to the saw. If you sit things get nasty. This goes in here."

Again, his fingertip traced about the tip of the knife, nudging my labia apart, spreading my wetness. Him doing that, toying with me, with his other hand on my ass...I gulped. There was fear and there was what he created, a mix of lust, control, and the evilest thing imaginable.

Would he cut me? I didn't know. A whimper escaped my lips.

I heard the rasp of cloth as he stood.

"Don't bite." A second later, he wormed two fingers into my mouth, past my teeth, then he hooked them into my cheek, casually holding me.

His lower hand dragged moisture from the knife tip all the way to my clit. He began to play...games – stroking my clit, toggling it back and forth, pinching it until I yelped, then playing some more. My eyes rolled back.

My arousal burgeoned into an impending climax.

I grabbed the rope that led above my hands and twined my fingers into the strands until the pain from that agonized. I wouldn't come. I wouldn't move. Mustn't.

Except, he could make me.

The tension built, until I thought I'd burst if I held back. I sucked bubbly air past his thick fingers, my hips thrusting back and forth by micro fractions.

Remember. The blade. Remember.

I was going to come apart.

Any. Fucking.

Second.

"If you come," he said, from close by, and I heard his feet shift. "If." Then his mouth was on mine, despite his fingers still occupying my mouth. I felt the movements of his lips as he formed words. "I get to punish. I think that's fair."

He squashed finger and thumb onto my clit, held it. I moaned, impossibly close...

Too late. I jerked and gargled some impossible reply as I came onto the knife, with him inside my mouth, inside my mind, holding my clit, and watching as I unraveled into the devastation of orgasm. *Fuck. Him.*

My knees almost gave way but I straightened, swallowing drool as his fingers left me. Twitching and more than a little undone with the aftershocks, I managed to stay where he'd put me though my head flopped back.

The stars were up there. But my eyes stayed shut.

I wasn't cut.

"You came."

I had.

Which meant...

I heard the crunch of his feet.

A swish through the air warned me...

CHAPTER 10

Wolfe

One stroke.

Her scream when the plastic strut whipped across her ass made me stop and stare, then step away. Her sobbing lasted so long.

Orgasm then pain. Or pain then orgasm. It did it for me.

For her too. She couldn't hide that, not from me.

I unbuttoned, unzipped, and took off my jeans and boxers. My shirt had gone long before, before she shrieked, before her body stiffened and came with my hands on her. She'd almost bitten me.

Before.

This was going to be good. I walked around her, my blind and sobbing girl, knowing I had forever to do what I wanted. All night. I could make her come and scream and come again.

If anyone else was camped nearby, I'd find out soon. The sound would carry.

If anyone arrived, I'd make her say she was happy and fine.

She was mine to do with as I wanted.

I sat on one of the other blocks of weed-grown brickwork, with the strut across my thighs and my hand wrapped around my erection. From here, only a few yards away, the wheal on her butt stood out plain.

When I rose and walked closer, around to her front, she turned her head, following the sound of my footsteps. I knelt before the pile of my clothes and slid the belt from my jeans. One hand held the strut, the other the tinkling belt. The buttons of her areolas had flattened though her nipples had stayed erect, as had her little clit. Tempting.

"You wondering what I'm doing next? Or if I'm done?"

Hesitant, she nodded.

"Good." I put the strut on the block near her, gathered the belt in my fist so only ten or so inches of it was free. I lashed one breast then the other. She jerked and her foot slipped from its place then recovered. Paleness showed on her skin before the blood rushing back pinked her skin.

Who needed floodlights when the moon showed me everything?

"Pretty." I squeezed the striped breast, taking a big handful.

She bit her lip but said nothing.

"Don't hold your breath. I won't be stopping soon."

I lashed them both for about twenty strokes. I wasn't precision counting. I was watching her jerk and squirm, her gasps, the little hops she almost made. I kept going, only I alternated and tapped or smacked the leather onto her clit every few strokes. Her mouth fell open. Her breathing became erratic.

Smiling, I swapped. I picked up the strut and applied it to her ass until it too was striped with red. It took a while before she got over the change in the hurting. Then she writhed and her stomach muscles twisted as the instinct to avoid pain reversed and sent her chasing it instead. She strived to keep her feet still but sometimes they slipped.

I stopped and found myself panting, same as she was. Fucking with her mind and body was good exercise.

Slumping into the rope, with her head lolling forward, and her hair across her face, Kiara struggled for air.

Oh god came out repeatedly, as if she was clockwork. When she wound down, I started again.

I whacked the belt across her mons. She jumped, moaning. I pressed my fingers into her pussy, working her higher with those as well as gripping her mind and making her face what I did. I think for a while she saw my fingers as I did, saw how destroyed she looked, how lost in the pain I'd made her.

I caught some of her moans in my mouth, kissing her lips, taking her there while my fingers penetrated her. I made a construct of lust, built it high, higher, then I stepped away...

Three well-placed strokes on her cunt and clit and she tensed and came, crying out as her body arched. Spittle shone in the moonlight, trailing from one corner of her mouth. Sweat sheened her skin and ran in thicker trails down her stomach.

When I stepped to her and dragged up one eyelid, her pupil was barely visible and had rolled into the top half. I released her eyelid and for a second she focused on me before her eye slowly shut.

"Think I'm done? Did that hurt?"

She gulped a few times then whispered, "Yessss."

But it was good too. That was a yes I didn't need to check on. Not that the hurting wasn't obvious.

"You dance well, but..."

I didn't want her falling.

I let her go, then I retrieved some more rope and four tent pegs. I hammered them into the earth and roped her ankles, tying them so she couldn't close her legs, couldn't open them much either.

Now, I could really do what I wanted. She was red most places — belly, breasts, ass, upper back. Nothing wrong with painting her in deeper red.

I heaved in a few lungfuls and wiped away the sweat on my face with the back of my forearm. Then I gave my cock a few languid strokes.

Not to be fucked? Was I sure of that?

Everything I'd brought with me made a long row on the grassed area. A whippy branch plucked smooth. The strut. The belt, laid out like a dead snake. A dozen bulldog clamps from a stack of folders the woman had piled in the back seat.

Should I be doing this? The question lay before me, accusing. I shouldn't.

My head filled with such a dire craving. No man could deny his nature.

I closed my eyes then opened them on a sight that swept away sense — Kiara, bound to the huge beam above her, that spanned from one wall of the saw mill to the next. Below her, the block. There was no saw. I'd made that up. An ancient, rusty saw seethed of threat, of teeth, of cutting, of blood spilled and agony. The knife was the bent-over end of a shiny tent peg that was tied to a baseball bat. The woman with the BMW must've had kids. I'd wedged the thick end of the bat into a slot in the middle of the block.

I went to her and took away the baseball bat. I put my hand on her hip, marveling at how perfect she was. How well she writhed at the scrape of my nails as I circled her.

Moonlight cascaded down her body, lighting her up in coruscations of startling red and pink and blue. I tasted her sweat, took a mouthful of the flesh at her hip and bit, then another of her ass. I painted her with her own orgasmic cum, fed her some on my fingers, and whispered sweet threats as I fastened some of the clamps. I listened to her cute whimpers. Then I whipped her again with my arsenal and watched the rise of the colors in the air around her. They worshipped her as I did. The flecks and motes caressed her until she became a goddess of pain, a dancer, a supplicant who begged me to stop making her twitch and writhe, to stop her coming.

Her scent overrode all.

I lapped her sweat and bit her feet, tasting the grit mixed with faint traces of her blood. I delved into her cunt with fingers and implements, relishing the wet sounds as I fucked her with them. My cock throbbed when she screamed for me to stop, and it throbbed when she begged me to *never* stop.

The scenery spun around the female.

I slashed the ropes and let her down and she lay over the block, belly down and gasping. Her cunt lay open to me, swollen and ready. I pulled her down to the grass, arranged her ass, spread her wide. And I dragged her onto my cock, feeling her cunt strain to take me. I fucked her while the moon laughed. I lay over her and pulled out, then prodded her other hole with my cunt-moistened dick until it too, slowly, let me in.

My cock sank into her until all of it was swallowed and inside her asshole. When she scrambled to rise on hands and knees and crawl away, I growled. Then, I began to fuck her properly.

CHAPTER 11

Kiara

My mind was full of fucking sounds and my ass was full of cock.

This should've bothered me. I knew that. Yesterday, I'd been a nurse, a carer, a person to respect. Now...

He withdrew completely, then fed himself into my ass again and I lost track of logic as he forged deeper. That appreciation for being taken how and where he wanted to, rippled into me, pushing up the volume, plugging into whatever place in me arranged for orgasms.

He'd given me fire and pleasure and more pain until I was a jigsaw person shattered into a million pieces.

I tried to crawl from him, instinctively, in self-preservation. His cock had pulled all of an inch out of me when he growled a warning. I shuddered to a stop. Body aching, stinging, flaring with pain in places uncountable, I stuck my ass out for more.

Wolfe gave it.

He hauled back my hair, gripped the front of my throat in his other hand, and fucked me.

Grass scored my knees, my palms. Then he twisted my hair and pulled my head back until I knew he was meeting my eyes.

"Look at me." The words sounded rough enough to scrape his throat raw.

I opened my eyes, for the first time in what seemed hours. So dark, but I could see his eyes and they never left mine, his focus obsessed, despite his cock shoving in and out. My arms were outstretched and clawing at the ground before me, as I strove to stay in place and not be driven into the ground.

Sweat dribbled down the sides of my face and soaked my back. His skin slid across mine in that incessant rhythm.

"Don't make me come," I choked out. I'd begged him before.

This time, though immersed in his pleasure, he seemed to hear.

I was rocked and hammered back and forth, and each thrust filled my ass with what seemed an impossible amount of cock.

He lowered his head and took a bite of my shoulder, grunting, as if the mouthful of my flesh pleased him. The last few, flesh-slapping thrusts banged into me. As his cock swelled, I braced myself with a new handful of grass and earth. I could feel it, feel him about to come, and my pussy seemed far too empty. Then he shoved in one last time, pushing my face to the grass, flattening me as he climaxed.

Done. I blinked through stunned eyes.

Surely, now, this would end?

Nothing had ever come close to this, ever, in my entire life.

What was I to think or to feel after so many orgasms had been forced on me? After he'd whipped me, made me hurt, given me the most incredible orgasms? Was it punishment or some depraved, distorted gift?

I couldn't...think. No one could have. Weary, we sank into sleep together, dirty and cum-smeared, wrapped limb over limb, and he was still inside me.

Caring about this or wondering, it could wait. I couldn't leave anyway. Best...to sleep.

When he began to lick me, I came awake for only enough seconds to understand what was happening. Smiling, though hazy as to the why, I let my eyes close.

By the time he stirred, pulled me upright, and dragged me away by the hand, I'd recovered some awareness though I was bleary-eyed and stumbling.

"Where are we going?" I croaked.

He stared back, ferocious in demeanor, yet silent. I tried again.

The man holding my hand seemed unwilling or unable to speak. Half my skin felt as if it had been flayed and stuck back on — almost true. From predator and torturer, he'd become, what? My patient again?

How to deal with this?

Gently, I encouraged him to talk but he said nothing. Without drugs, did Wolfe regress until he forgot how to use language? I couldn't figure that one out, not at this time of night.

Pretend he's a patient.

"I have to pee." Embarrassed, I mimed it too. His huff seemed the best reply I'd get.

I walked away and he watched me go, then went off to a nearby spot and, from the sounds, also urinated. On my return, I found my handbag and retrieved a dose of Keppra while he stood a yard away.

My hands shook. His eyes fixed on my every move, but he said nothing.

Okay. How did I get him to take it?

"Drink? Eat?" I mimed again, feeling silly to do this before him when hours before he'd been sane and normal.

And in between he'd been my monster lover.

Instead he pointed at the sleeping bags and dragged me down to them. Lying on my side with the pills clutched in hand and under my chin, I waited while he arranged the sleeping bag so it covered us both.

What would happen if he never recovered? I could manipulate him while he was like this – Neanderthal-like. Or perhaps not. There seemed no humanity in him. He might kill me or maim me and not even see the consequences.

I had to get this into him.

Wolfe slurped his tongue across my neck, grumbling as he molded his body to my back. His heavy arm was draped over my chest and I could feel him growing hard again. My pussy was so sore, I prayed he'd sleep. The licking continued and it dawned on me what to do. Quietly, but quickly, I chewed at the tablet until I had the soggy remains in my palm. Then I reached back and smeared the drug over where he licked me.

Gross, but necessity was the mother of doing stuff that was gross.

After one lick he grunted and stopped. *Dayum.* A moment later, he gripped my breast and his cock prodded at me, found my entrance, and slid inside.

I gasped at the initial sting of my abused flesh being stretched.

His lovemaking was surprisingly gentle and almost an afterthought. I was so exhausted, with my skin throbbing in time with my heartbeats, and so tired of being scared and unsure that being fucked like this sent me floating. He thrust into me slowly and within a minute I felt his tumescence increase, his rhythm become harder, faster, then the pressure of his cum injecting into me.

It had to be how he handled me, that way he could make me do stuff, but...yeah, that'd felt good, and I smiled drowsily.

Oops and fuck. I mustn't sleep yet. He'd not taken the drug. The stuff was bitter. What might entice him? Something to overcome that nasty taste?

Chocolate or beer or whiskey or a hundred other things weren't anywhere within reach. I could only think of one possibility that was within reach. One thing that might attract him. Icky, but, if it worked...

I wrinkled my nose then reached down between my legs and collected some of the natural moisture there, then I attempted to mix it with the paste of the tablet. The things one did when desperate.

He snuffled at my neck, then began licking me again. *Yesss. Oh, yes.* The relief, that hopefully he would be more normal soon, let me relax. How strangely erotic his licking could be. I shifted my neck, murmured an appreciative noise, and let myself succumb to the pleasure of having a man warming me with the heat of his body.

In the middle of the night, I woke with a start. He slept beside me, on his back and I sneaked a glance his way. Snoring. Oblivious that I watched him. I wanted him normal again but, if he remembered the pills...I could be in trouble in the morning.

And what had that been about, before, snuggling up to the man who'd just beaten me? Even so...my skin didn't crawl at that piece of delivered fact. I liked being near him, and that was so...so...

Ugh. I squashed shut my eyes. *Does not compute.*

It took a while before sleep again claimed me.

CHAPTER 12

Damian

Their UAV sitting in the hands of the park ranger was a minus, but Damian dismissed disappointment with a twitch of his mouth and pretended to listen to the lecture – they had another drone in the boot anyway.

"You folks have violated a regulation we've had in force since last year. Be best if you check up on such things next time. It'd avoid this happening." He slammed the trunk of his car. "You understand you won't be getting it back?"

He and Guera nodded.

"Yes, sir," he added. Always best to placate authorities and act average. "Sorry. I really am."

"Just sign here to acknowledge that the matter has been explained to you and you accept the penalty and we're all good." The ranger offered the clipboard with the form on it, all filled out with date, their car registration, and their fake names. Then he waited, hands on hips, while Damian signed.

"Thank you, ma'am, sir. Have a good day, won't you."

"We sure will." Damian kept the smile on his face until the ranger had disappeared up the road.

"Nice man," Guera mused.

"He was. We didn't even have to shoot him."

"As if we would." Guera mock punched his arm. "So. We drive on for a bit longer before starting up drone two?"

"I think so. That seems wise. Getting caught twice would look bad. I'm not sure how he found us either."

"Well, we have their general direction as they exited this area. The highway. Going west. I wish we knew what he might be aiming for there. With luck and the tracer, we can pick them up again."

"Yes. Yes. I hope so." He rubbed his chin. "I'm going to ask for clarification. Since he's driving, he may have something from his past making him want to go that way."

"Great idea. And now that you mention it, your turn to drive."

When they reached their Ford, he grabbed Guera and pinned her to the door, squeezing her with his body, then leaning in to capture her mouth.

The kiss went on for some time before they came up for air.

"Damnation." She exhaled then reached up to put her thumb to his mouth. Damian sucked it in and bit down.

"Owww. Now you are *really* turning me on." She slowly extracted her thumb from his teeth, giggling as she did so. "I wish we had time to go make love."

"Not yet." Damian stepped away, though he took her hand and kissed her fingers. "Soon. Once we catch him."

"We must be quick then." She tossed him the keys.

CHAPTER 13

Kiara

When I shifted the sleeping bag off my face, morning shone, full blast, into my eyes.

Two wild turkeys were rustling about in the undergrowth at the edge of this clearing, scratching up dirt and leaves, and Wolfe was...

I peeked around, turned over, and found him munching on a bowl of cereal. Milk splattered in a messy waterfall into his bowl with every spoonful he lifted and he chewed with his mouth open half the time.

I wrinkled my nose and muttered, "Manners," before I could put a brake on my tongue, before I remembered last night and why my back and butt hurt. Why everywhere hurt if I sat on it.

He was glaring. Had he heard?

I tried to cover up with the sleeping bag again but then did a suicidal reverse backflip on that idea. Instead, I threw off the bag and stood, though a few moves had me wincing. His glare changed into an appreciative, slow cruise down my body.

Of course. I was naked.

Damn. I shut my eyes for a second then opened them.

He wasn't prowling for me and that was intelligence in his eyes. This was like the gunfight at the OK Corral. Neither of us moved and he recommenced munching on and swallowing cereal. Had he forgotten last night? It was possible. I couldn't know unless I asked, and I sure wasn't doing that.

It might be best if I simply acted as if nothing had happened.

"Morning." I turned and headed for the bag with my clothes.

It wasn't until I had my hands full of bra, panties, and a skirt and top that he spoke.

"Come here."

Well fuck. That spoiled it. After one somewhat shaky breath, I headed over, clothes clutched in hand.

"What?" I halted a few feet away from where he sat on the log, and cocked an eyebrow.

No way was I subjugating myself to him. I didn't care what he did. Had done.

A memory flashed in of his hands all over me while I came, of my body not my own, tied up and at his will. It had been...what? Demeaning? Yes, but also, there'd been the rush of a climax tempered with pain singing across my body in a thousand, amazing places.

I swayed and came back to the present.

"How are you?" He put the bowl of cereal on the ground and leaned forward, his focus moving from place to place on my body even as his hands reached for me. "Bruises." He pressed here and there, on breast, stomach, and thigh. I hissed and flinched though he held me in place. "Marks." The tone of his voice was almost reverent. "Turn."

I turned and again felt the brush of his skin on mine. Surprisingly, he was gentle. When he rested one hand on my hip while the other hand journeyed, palm down, over my ass, one cheek then the other, my breathing deepened – my body reacting without my damn permission.

It was...nice, having him do this. I was a project he oversaw, a test bunny, but more personal than that, much more personal. I held my breath when he slid that palm between my legs and left it there, cupped over my pussy. The world drifted.

"I don't remember everything I did to you last night. It wasn't moral or legal, but I'm not sorry."

Was this surprising? No.

I swallowed as he continued in that low, deliberate tone. There were reactions I should be having. Tears to shed. Indignant, angry words. But, as it was, with him holding me, nothing was worth doing because it would interrupt the intense sensation he'd conjured. In that moment, I belonged to him and everything else could wait.

In the blurred distance, the turkeys kept doing what turkeys did. The sun shone through the trees and, as leaves and branches shook in a breeze, the light flickered, shifted, bright as the purest gemstones.

"Not because you deserved it," he continued in that soothing monotone. "Because I liked doing it – making you like something you'd never ask for in a million years. Would you?"

His thumb delved along my slit then he casually popped it inside. My toes curled the instant he entered me and I couldn't help sighing.

It was equally immoral to like this. Had he asked a question? I wasn't facing him so I would just refuse to answer.

"That was a real question."

Crap.

"Would I?"

"Ask for it."

"No."

"No? I'll have to change that." After working his thumb in and out enough times that my pussy was making embarrassing wet sounds and I was biting my lip to stop myself squeaking, he pulled it out.

His wet thumb made a cooling trail up my backbone to end at my neck, where he drew a line across the base. Something scratched me there. "What's this, Kiara?"

His voice seemed to come from the bottom of a deep well. I summoned my mind, blinking and trying to figure out what he meant. I put my hand to my neck. There was something circling my neck.

"Grass?" I frowned.

"Yes. Did I put it there?" He used his hands to turn me to face him.

It felt like the lightest of necklets, a twined chain of grass leaves and seed heads. Had he? If so, I'd been asleep.

I shrugged.

The corner of his mouth sneaked upward. Amusement lines surrounded his blue eyes. "Guess I did. Keep it there. Until it falls off."

Huh. I shrugged again.

"Say yes." He pinched my clit between finger and thumb.

Startled, blitzed into arousal, I stared open-mouthed. He increased the pressure and I blurted, "Yes!"

"Good girl. Go get dressed. We're leaving in ten."

What? I hadn't had time to eat. We had to pack...and what was this? Was I organizing a family picnic? Who gave a flying fuck if we were late leaving? I slouched toward the sleeping bag area and began slowly dressing.

"Ten," he repeated. "Or else."

I looked at him. The *or else* had made my nipples perk up and a chill chase through my body.

Wait, he could have just made this a true order. Or was that too easy? He had preferences, as he'd said about last night, such as the application of sticks and other things I hadn't even seen —

"I could've made everything hurt more, much more, if I'd wanted to."

Mind reader.

I hurried to dress.

* * * * *

We wound our way through the forest then out the other side, heading west, from the direction of the dawn.

I stared out the window, at the vehicles passing, at my toenails, and I wondered if I should paint them...if I survived.

"Where are we going?"

"The Iron Range area, Minnesota. I have a friend there."

"Ahh." Trees and farmland flowed past my window. The day was overcast but bright enough to make the swathes of dandelions by the roadside seem yellow enough to pop. "You did say that."

I snuggled into the angle of door and seat and eyed him, dubiously. Every bounce of the car made me ache. Lucky it was a BMW with good suspension.

Staying quiet and ignorant might've been wise, but look at me — agreeing to be a spy in the USA just so I could get back here. Clearly, wise wasn't a big part of my make-up.

How long ago had this friend of Wolfe's lived there? I thought of asking, but he likely wouldn't know. Besides, being his captive didn't mean helping him by encouraging him to remember. A nurse, yes, but not now.

Unless he ordered me too.

Yeah, that.

Don't run away again. Don't do anything I wouldn't like. That one was so vague I could maybe dodge it, if I thought it through? Or was it just some bone-deep understanding of the meaning of his words? In which case, I was up creek minus paddle.

I had this horrible urge to ask him very pointed questions, though. He'd made me *feel* things last night... I had to know.

I should hold my tongue.

"Why'd you hit me last night?" There. Asked it anyway.

In trepidation, I waited.

He kept his concentration on the highway.

"I like it."

"So you said."

"That's not enough?"

The bastard was smiling and here I was squirming over asking a question and I couldn't even figure out why I'd had to ask it.

"No."

"I like it. I think...I've always liked it. But only if the lady also wants it."

What? Well, that ruled out –

"Did you like it?"

This being new...

Did *I* like it?

I blinked, thinking furiously. "You know this doesn't make for a sensible answer. I guess I did...but only because you made me."

"You liked it." Finally, he glanced at me. "And do you want more?"

Now I knew why I should never ever have touched this topic. My throat felt filled with glue, yet I knew that in a few damning seconds I'd be answering.

He just waited and the pressure of that question built.

If I said yes, what did it mean? Still, he could compel me to do anything. So my feelings meant nothing.

Really.

I swallowed down that gluey chunk of squeamishness, and despite the nausea saying these next words brought on, I uttered a "Yes."

The car purred onward and neither of us spoke. Was he letting me stew on my answer, or had he lost interest? I wouldn't look his way and find out.

The roadside flowers got bucket loads of attention.

We stopped that night at a motel, after Wolfe reconnoitered and found out the receptionist was susceptible to his control. No sign-ins, no payment exchanged hands, nothing. When we left, they'd clean our room and it would be as if we'd never been here at all. How was anyone going to find me? I'd tried not to fret but I wasn't superwoman.

I could end up dead. Wolfe wasn't entirely sane. Okay, worse, at times he was barely human.

The TV had showed a short, news story of a missing patient, Wolfe, and the nurse who seemed to have kidnapped him – me. If I could've simply walked into the local restaurant attached to this motel, I could've been free of Wolfe.

He'd forbidden me to run and that was it.

Stuck here, with him, for one more night.

With two single beds. I rolled onto my stomach and bunched the pillow under my chin and chest, shut my eyes. I'd managed to get a partial dose into him with the take-out he'd had brought to us, so I wasn't concerned about him going nuts, not tonight.

What if I managed a heavy dose and made him sink into an Andy-type status? Would that give me leave to escape? He'd implied some orders would last and last. I should try it.

I didn't owe him. With all the evidence on my body, the bruises and scratches, they'd prosecute him not me.

The bed sank at the edge and I realized Wolfe was here and he'd put his knee on the bed, plus most of his body weight. When he pulled the sheet off my lower back then rolled my panties down to the top of my thighs, dread and anticipation arrived, in equal proportions.

Equal. *Fuck*.

"Want this?" His hand rested on my ass – such a large, male hand, weighty with the promise of sex, and I swear I could smell his presence.

I stayed with my eyes buried in the pillow and my arms. Maybe I was crazy too.

A *yes* would set off the avalanche. Saying no would be a lie and I could already feel the resistance of speaking a falsehood waiting in my throat.

I couldn't lie, but would my answer be mine, or one he'd subtly arranged?

I didn't know.

And I didn't *really* care. How easily I betrayed myself. There was a halfway answer that I could use.

"Maybe," I said softly, kind of hoping he'd not hear me.

"Maybe?"

He leaned in and sank his teeth into my ass then two fingers into my pussy.

"Fuck!" I gripped the pillow tighter.

The unrelenting pain blasted away my doubts, leaving me stuck in the now, where a man called Wolfe was appropriating my body to use how he wanted to. He hooked his fingers deeper and used them to lift my lower body then drop me again to the bed.

Stunned, I sobbed, almost, *almost* ready to spread my legs and beg.

"Answer properly." This time his tone was dead mean.

I panted into the pillow then threw myself into his path by blurting, "Yes!" I prayed he'd not hurt me too much. "Yes."

Not trust, just prayer. I didn't know if I could ever trust him.

"Good."

By the time I came, I had several new, throbbing teeth marks all over my ass and back. Some, I feared might be bleeding. But when he sank his cock into me, I merely held onto the sheets and suffered, and enjoyed the ride.

He dragged the beds together afterward and wrapped me in his body, while I stayed sprawled in limbo, across most of my own bed. Breathing, just breathing. How bizarre this was.

If only this was real. If only he was a lover and not...whatever he was. I had to remember not to trust him.

"Your grass necklace is gone."

"Mmm."

I felt the bed rock as he climbed out.

"Guess I'll have to make do with this." A moment later, his belt was cinched around my neck – not tight though. Then he settled behind me again and grunted in satisfaction. Drowsily, I put my hand up to feel the leather. I could tell his hand held the loose end, between us and partway down my back.

"Sleep."

I snorted softly and heaved in a breath with my nose in the fresh scent of the pillow. Already, I was going...my eyelids became heavier and I exhaled...

There...

CHAPTER 14

Wolfe

The drive had wearied both of us. I'd made her drive while I napped and vice versa, but two days of being in the car for over twelve hours each day had been sapping. Avoiding being seen by surveillance cameras, or anyone I couldn't control, had made my mind slowly turn to mush.

It wasn't easy, though I never let on to Kiara.

I'd stolen gas, food, motel rooms, and most of all, people's sanity. Some of them would have explaining to do with their spouses, though I'd tried to minimize the splash impact of my manipulations. Best to stay close to invisible.

Just using the BMW for several days made me uncomfortable.

Could I make that woman be quiet and never tell she'd gifted away a vehicle like this? I prayed so, but I wasn't certain.

We'd gone near the lift bridge at Duluth a few hours back. A massive ship had passed beneath after the whole damn bridge lifted above it. It'd impressed on me how petty my life was, how much I owed due to simply being alive.

Once upon a time, everyone had seemed to want me dead.

The bullets had left me shattered and the pieces were still coming together. One bullet had gone into my brain. Yet I was here. I wasn't normal, like Kiara said, and I wasn't sure I wanted all those pieces back.

People screamed and turned into blood in some.

Details were elusive, but feelings ate their way through into my head: the awful loneliness, the hunger, the desperate need to survive. How long had I been in that pit? Memories gave hints but the worst scenes were in darkness. Maybe it was all imagination, scoured from some place in me that brought nightmares not truth?

Maybe I just thought I'd been in Hell because half my brain had been turned to mush.

A man just didn't grow that back. What the fuck was I?

I shook my head, gripping the wheel with white-knuckled hands, then I realized my hair had stayed in place. I smiled grimly. Kiara had helped tie it together.

Currently, she snored gently with her head in a pillow wedged to the door.

She wanted me to let her go.

The faintest smile formed on her lips despite the unladylike snore. Every time I saw her, I yearned to sketch her again, in a million different poses – in some she'd be the most precious and fragile girl ever, sprawled in a sea of flowers or washed by a stream. In others...she'd be tied up and at my mercy...or at the mercy of a vile-toothed monster with a blood-streaked body, and a blood-streaked whip in his hand, and spikes, and all manner of shiny evil instruments. And she writhed before that monster, chained and leashed to a pole.

I shifted to relieve the pressure on my cock. Letting her go was definitely not a priority.

I slowed and pulled over to the side of the road to take a break. The mountain soared to the heavens from the earth ahead. Even through the windshield, I could feel the drop in temperature. Never was there anywhere that felt so clean and pure as being high on a mountain with a cold wind in your face and nature abounding.

I'd loved this when I'd come here in the past. This freedom to think away from pressure and people must be why I'd felt the urge to come. Why the memories had surfaced. The cabin owned by Magnus was half fallout shelter, half ode to nature. Solid. It'd be up here still, even if he wasn't home. I couldn't recall much about the man but he'd been a close friend, and his main abode was in New York.

That memory had come back. Others would too, given time, peace, a safe place where no one could disturb me.

The little town of Ely wasn't too far – down a road on the other side of the cabin. I'd go there after I'd found how the cabin had weathered the years – leave Kiara behind with instructions and go get some supplies. I'd be careful and not take too much from whoever I chose.

I closed the door of the BMW carefully, trying not to wake Kiara. Bees flitted past. The scent of the flowers and the tang of leaves and dirt was strong. Something big floundered through the bushes on the opposite side of the road, where the slope dropped away. Bear or moose, perhaps.

Peeing on flowers seemed wrong, so I aimed at the tufts of grass instead.

I'd get well here. I knew it.

This small road was narrow and flanked by scrub and scattered cascades of wildflowers. I'd parked the BMW so as to leave room for others to pass, which made it surprising when a white sedan pulled up behind us. I zipped up and turned, wondering if they thought us broken down.

Only to face a gun pointed at my face. The bearded, red-eyed man, in faded jeans and hunter's jacket, had a wobble to his gun-aiming arm.

"Don't say a fucking word!" he rattled off, spit flying.

I halted, raised my hands.

His girlfriend sauntered along behind, long blond hair wisping in the breeze. Her swagger gave the impression she enjoyed this. One hand was hooked in her waistband and the other was wrapped around a second pistol that she dangled at her side. A Glock.

Her fidgety boyfriend had a Beretta.

I had nothing except me. It'd do.

"Hmm?" I raised my eyebrows.

"Keys. Hand them over. And get her out!" He pointed through the window then whacked the glass. "Tell her if she grabs anything she gets shot. Then you."

And he'd just said don't speak.

The keys were in the car but he seemed too jittery to notice.

Girlfriend grinned and raised her gun. Her red-edged eyes matched those of her boyfriend's. As did the track marks on her arm. Her pink T-shirt had *F##ck me, do I care?* emblazoned across the front. "Yeah. Money, keys, your girl, your car, if you wanna live."

Her sneer was a work of art as deep as her T-shirt words.

Kiara must've heard, plus the guy tapped the glass again with his gun and aimed it at her, at me, at her, at me again. Indecisive bastard.

I pulled open the door to let her climb out and backed away as she did so, going right and a little closer to the guy, to widen the area he'd need to cover. His aim wibble-wobbled between us.

"On yer knees!" He spat. "Both of you. Woooo. What a preeetty girl you got."

All the while, I grappled for the right signs in his girl's mind, or lack of mind. I needed her. I could kick the shit out of her boyfriend but someone would get shot. Maybe Kiara.

Kneeling would make it hard to move fast enough.

Kiara was shuffling to her knees, with her hands up.

"Now!" His Beretta muzzle grafted to me.

Girlfriend raised her gun too, but she left that other hand on hip in a casual, we-can-both-fuck-you-up way. If she fired, she'd likely hurt her teensy wrist.

"Now!" he screamed again. "Do it now!"

"Ooo, Greebo. Love it when you're mad."

I bent one knee as if about to obey.

He twitched a grin in her direction. "You ain't seen nothing, yet, baby. This slow-as-fuck cocksucker just made me decide to get her to suck my cock." He nodded at Kiara, his grin widening. I'd paused in movement. "Still slow! Do it, you fucker!"

I pretended I was confused, though at most it would give me a few seconds. Then I didn't care anymore.

Things *clicked*.

I had her sidestep nearer to the car, kink the gun around to aim at him with a slight upward angle. I didn't want blood on the car or us. She fired. *Boom* and brains blew out spray-splattering the shrubs and the road surface with liquid gobbets. Color – red.

He flatlined to the road, puddling and bleeding.

Kiara screamed. The girl mugger screamed and clutched her wrist. Knew it.

Though she sobbed, I had the girl walk into the bushes. Once she was knee-deep in plants, she raised the gun, put the muzzle to her mouth, and slid it in. Cross-eyed, she fixated on the gun.

The hate inside her...I couldn't let her live, even if I could stop her telling. Possibilities of doom ratcheted past – she mightn't keep her mouth shut; forensics, if fresh, might find something. What though?

Didn't have time to figure that. Needed to get this done before someone else arrived. Their car was here too. Leave it. Leave it and don't touch a *thing*.

Number one future possibility, the one that spun in circles in my thoughts, was her finding Kiara and killing her. That wouldn't be right.

It would be disastrous.

Kiara turned her head and looked at me, eyes wide with fear and disbelief.

I sent the command.

CHAPTER 15

Kiara

I could see in his eyes that he meant to follow through.

My *nooo* came at the same instant as the gunshot and I turned to see her falling, straight down, as if her knees had been severed. She vanished into the bushes. Gone, bar for the spray of blood spattering down like rain. Then there was him, the man, heaped on the road with a pool of red surrounding what was left of his skull.

"You didn't have to." I gulped.

"I did. You didn't see in her mind."

Fuck no, I didn't. Funny that. I shut my eyes, climbing to my feet by feel with my hand on the car. He'd killed two people so easily. And her? I understood having to kill the man but her? She'd been an ugly fool but she didn't have to die.

"She didn't have to die." Like, if I repeated it enough, maybe she might resurrect from the bushes.

It wasn't her hate-filled mind, it was Wolfe. He hadn't wanted us discovered.

"Get in the car."

Wolfe's hand on my elbow made me flinch and I shook him off.

"In."

This time it was a compulsion and I mounted the step and hoisted myself in despite my shaking hands and legs.

He climbed in the other side, started the engine, and we rolled forward.

"You're not..." I blinked and looked over. "Not hiding them."

"Best to make it look like it was just them. She killed him, then herself. Less fuss that way."

"Uh-huh." Whatever was out there, past the windshield, I didn't see it for a while.

Just seen two people die. I mean...I'd seen death many times, but this was different. Making someone else die just because you could and it was convenient? Jesus.

My knees were all strangely squished-in from kneeling on the road. That was the sum total of *my* injuries. I ran my fingers over my right knee, remembering how cold it was outside. I'd need jeans up here. Sweaters. Though my goosebumps and shivering wasn't just from the weather.

"They would've shot us, or done worse to you."

"What?" I mumbled. He glanced at me then went back to watching the road. "Made me give him a BJ? I could've survived that. Hell, you think you're better? You could've twisted her mind until she was Mother Theresa's clone."

"No. I can't do that."

"The hell you can't. God. *Fuck*." I hit the dashboard with my fist. Useless, this was all so useless. *I* felt useless.

"Swearing doesn't change anything. Stop doing it."

"Or what?" I blurted. My scowl deepened.

"Do you really want to find out?"

His matter-of-fact tone, combined with what I'd just seen him do, made me pause, but...he was driving and couldn't do anything.

"Fuck you," I grumbled.

I may have been suicidal saying that to him, a man who killed as if it were no fancier than sucking a lollipop, but I was past caring. If he'd wanted to shoot me, he'd had plenty of opportunities.

I'd abducted him, nearly sold him to the Russians. I'd also been his carer for months, and I'd liked him, once. Helped him. Now? I didn't know. It was all too raw and it hurt my chest to think about what had happened.

I shifted my butt, finally remembered to fasten the seat belt, then planted my head into the headrest.

They were dead as dead could be. Wolfe was right, I couldn't change anything. I should try to sleep. But always there were questions. What if the other agents turned up? If riled, Wolfe would happily go beyond the limits of the law or an average person's morals. Who would end up dead?

I had an inkling he'd chew them up and spit them out then keep on walking, as if nothing had happened.

CHAPTER 16

Wolfe

"We're going to stay here a while, until I figure things out."

Kiara hadn't spoken since I'd killed the two muggers. I didn't exactly blame her. That'd be traumatic for most, maybe even more so for a nurse. Didn't change why I did it or my feelings. I did it because they needed killing.

The place...this was Magnus's, for sure. I'd remembered the road in, even if it mostly petered out the last hundred yards and I'd had to forge through the overgrown shrubs while keeping a close eye on the ground. Only thing that'd saved this from being swallowed by trees was that much of it was on bedrock and the plants were growing in thin soil. I parked the SUV under some trees and nose-in to a heavy growth of some green shrub.

On the outside, the cabin looked ready to fall over the edge of the mountain that was ten yards to the left. Brick and timber construction, and a roof that had a few bits of trees collapsed over it.

"Looks done for." Her first words for ages.

"Magnus was a survivalist. This is made to look old. Built on the shell of an abandoned cabin. Behind that is new brick and some concrete."

I peered through the glass of the windshield one last time before popping open the door and slipping out. A raccoon scampered down a rotten tree trunk that lay propped at the right corner of the cabin, then ran off.

In the last shine of daylight, some of the leafless branches looked golden. Parts were starting to lift off, like scales barely adhering to skin. They shook, eager to float.

That...not good.

I needed food. It seemed to stave off the signs of the crazies.

The front door had tons of leaves and crap piled up to it. I ripped away some dangling plants and bent on one knee. Memories said the key was under all this. Under the welcome mat...which was probably not here anymore.

"What, are you doing?"

"Welcome mat." I tunneled my hand down through dirt, more dirt, then some roots, and found the edge of something synthetic, which I flapped about to loosen then ripped up and out. The wonders of modern science. I had an entire green, still *bright* green, mat in my hand.

"You're joking? Way up here in the beyond... He has a key under a mat?"

"Yup." Metal found my hand, a ring of it. Which meant... I dragged the metal out through the loosened soil. Triumphant, I held up the key.

"Incredible."

At least she was talking.

I straightened and rubbed my forehead, keeping the colors at bay by concentrating hard. Then I ripped away the door, which fell to pieces. Behind was his real door. Metal. Somewhat rusted but solid. After I cleaned the key with rubbing, spit, and more spit and rubbing, I inserted it in the lock. A miracle, but it turned first go. After one shoulder-charge, the door swung in...revealing darkness.

"I need to get some food in me. Starting to feel odd."

The visions of blood and slaughtered women still spattered my waking hours, and my nightmares. I'd rather keep them at bay.

"Oh." The alarm in her eyes said it worried her as much as me. Guess she'd noticed. "I'll be back. Wait there."

"Bring a flashlight!"

I watched her ass as she ran back to the vehicle. Never failed to stir me – she had the perfect shape for groping, biting. Taking her down, stripping her, and fucking her from behind with leaf litter crunching under her, it'd be fun.

I *should* be checking the building.

The inside was clean of plant growth, no cracks in the ceiling, just dust and a lingering odor of smoke. All the heavy timbers up there in the roof had done the trick and stopped the weight of the debris from caving it in.

"So many years," I muttered. "And I can still smell smoke."

"I can't." Kiara was at my shoulder, checking out the interior too. "Are you sure? Come back to the SUV. I have some cans opened."

Maybe I imagined it. Smoke molecules wouldn't last that long.

We ate beans and canned sausages outside, sitting in the car, while swigging beer and bottled water to chase down the food.

"I'm going soon."

"What? Where?" She lowered her spoon. "It's nearly night."

"That's why I'm hurrying. I need to see the road and I have to find the secondary road into town. Can't use the one we came in on. The cops are likely there by now."

"You are going to leave me here? For how long? Hours?"

"All night. *Shhh.*" It was for the best. "The shutters need opening so I'll get the tire lever and shovel and knock them loose before I leave. But then I go. I want to get supplies and I can stay hidden down there even better at night."

I'd find someone with what I needed. Always easier not to be noticed at night. I'd walk into town from just outside and feel my way. "There'll be a woman I can use."

"Use?" She stilled. "But, you're leaving me here? At night. Without transport?"

I hopped out of the car. "You're not going anywhere anyway. You'll be fine. There's nothing up here that'll eat you. It'll be cold though."

"Damn right it will."

"Once in the house, go to sleep. I'll be back in the morning with food, a generator, whatever I can find." This would be a test, of sorts. May as well find out if she could disobey me. I didn't think she would, or could. "Don't go outside."

"Not even to pee? Jeez."

"For that, yeah, just be careful of the bogeyman."

Up here, getting lost on the mountain at night would be a sure way to die.

I'd be lucky not to drive off the cliff as it was, getting back down to a good road.

I had a flash vision of the SUV curving down over a great height, nose down, falling. Then another, of her here by herself, unable to leave, and slowly starving as the trees once more grew their tendrils and roots over the cabin, sealing her in.

Fun, fun, fun.

Evil was waiting to crack its way into me. I wouldn't let it in. Ever.

She'd be fine, I told myself, as I maneuvered through the scrubby plants clinging to life on the bedrock. I'd left her with plenty of warm bedding, the flashlight, and instructions to stay there and sleep until morning. There was nothing on this mountain that'd hurt a woman locked up in a house. Nothing except another man, like myself, and no one knew she was there.

CHAPTER 17

Kiara

Waking in the morning was a relief. His order to sleep had helped, but even so I'd packed a good amount of terror into the minutes before I finally succumbed. I'd thought about leaving anyway, for all of thirty seconds. However, going out there and falling off a precipice while stumbling around in the dark was not on my bucket list. Command or not.

Could I have done it? Slowly, I sat up and stared at the door where light managed to render it in an outline of searing yellow. The hinges and jamb had kept out the elements for many years, from the looks of this place, but light managed to sneak past the steel. And it was steel in parts, as if this Magnus had expected a rocket attack. I guess shit might happen during the next apocalypse but this'd be the last place to be visited by zombies.

That was probably the whole point.

I rolled out of bed, feeling the aches where the hard floor had dug in. Last night, looking around by flashlight had been enough to convince me there were no obvious monsters in here. Daylight made me want to explore further.

To the right of the door, where Wolfe had levered the shutters out a few inches, more shafts of light pricked at my eyes. Blearily, I staggered to my feet and stood listening.

Just bird noises out there, trees swishing and rattling branches, some creaking as the cabin stretched itself. Before eating me. *Haha.*

When would Wolfe be back? I had no idea. I just wished he'd be here soon, or else the medication would be so low in his blood that anything might happen. I hugged myself. The old flannelette shirt made me feel like some country hunter trapper hobo. The short shorts made my legs cold but if I put on some shoes, I'd be fine. Minus cold feet, I preferred wearing shorts. Unless the weather hit under fifty-five. Or I was running through things that'd scratch my legs...like down in the Pine Barrens.

That night would be forever scored into my mind.

I opened the door and stood shading my eyes and squinting a while. Nothing moved among the trees to the left, and the sky beckoned me with its blueness to the right where the land fell away to nothing. At least this place had been constructed on rock and wouldn't slide away in an avalanche...unless one started above. The mountain peak was behind the cabin. The tree line was far above this height, but it hadn't happened yet. The cabin was still here, after years, or so Wolfe thought.

How did he know how long it was since he'd been here? It could be a hundred years, if that were possible. The man was lost, no past, just the *now*. Unless he'd remembered a lot more and hadn't said?

My legs almost made me want to walk out there and keep going down the road. I tried a step, knew my bladder was full and I needed to pee. He'd said I could leave for that but what about more?

I edged another few steps onto the mostly grassless area. More? I stared down at my stupid unmoving legs. Apparently not. A line existed I couldn't cross.

Damn.

What if he died or got lost or arrested, or *anything* that meant he couldn't come back?

I'd be stuck here forever.

Shut up.

Shut up for god's sake.

I was spinning out a little here, feeling faint. I had to keep functioning. The ringing faded from my ears. I gulped once and centered myself, put my hand on my chest, as if to calm my thumping heart.

Okay, pee, then a breakfast of cereal, and that icky long-life milk, then... I could explore the cabin. I turned and looked into the interior, now quite illuminated from the light entering through the door.

Yes.

The shutters, big metal things, could be moved out some more too, though whatever shutters shielded the other windows would have to stay put – I'd seen the strength Wolfe had used to get the front ones to open. His biceps had bulged most impressively. Even his legs had thickened as he'd tensed and thrust into the ground to get a good position of strength.

The man...impressed me.

Scared me.

Did both sometimes. Shooting those two had been the worst. Even so, Wolfe didn't seem to plan to be destructive. Maybe I should truly listen and get his side of things and why he had done it?

Munching on corn flakes let me think through a few things. I sat with my back propped on the doorway, with the sleeping bag insulating my skin from the cold metal and the stone floor. The light washing in from the windows revealed the front room. A kitchen slash dining area.

It was all so caught in time – a bowl of shriveled fruit. A glass on the table. A butter knife on the floor. Someone had left in a hurry, perhaps. There might be other reasons.

I just liked postulating. Sherlock Holmes, eat my dust.

With the drug in him, Wolfe was still unpredictable. A bad man at times, yes. A homicidal crazy? He'd only killed when provoked, with guns in his face. That wasn't *bad* bad. What he'd done to me that night had been crazier. How many times had he made me come? Being scared *and* turned on had likely warped my memory. When I thought back, I could feel my arousal building. That was sick, wasn't it?

I couldn't even blame it on Stockholm Syndrome. It was just *him*.

"Fuck it." I scrambled upright, untangled from the sleeping bag, then placed the bowl and spoon just outside the door. Those needed cleaning and I had no idea how or where to get water. Apart from the drinking water.

I couldn't leave. I couldn't do what a normal person should do – run.

Okay. Be calm.

Nothing to be done, nowhere to go anyway. This was a desolate mountain in the middle of nowhere in Minnesota. Fine. I had the mind of a ferret or something. I loved poking around and figuring things out, and Wolfe had barely given me any info about this Magnus guy.

I wasn't going to find a phone here, but there might be something I could use?

I shut the door first – no use letting in some wild animal. Then I switched on my flashlight though I didn't need it yet.

This first room, that went the width of the cabin, held a wood-fired oven, a solid timber table, a long counter below the window, a sink with a faucet connected to a pipe – which meant water had to come from somewhere. I turned the faucet and nothing arrived, of course. The water had probably dried up long ago but maybe there was a tank somewhere? Strangely there was an electric light fitting, a bulb, in the ceiling, as well as an old oil lantern on the wall. I guessed that would've been fired with kerosene? My camping knowledge wasn't the best.

A door on the right led into a short, very dark hallway and I raised the flashlight, finding another door to the left leading into what seemed a living room. Here there were dusty, moldy couches, a table, a fireplace, and walls filled with books. Some of the books had toppled to the floor, others had been left in piles. If I'd been asthmatic, I'd have been wheezing by now. The mold and smoke smell was thick.

Being so closed-in must've preserved the smell.

The fireplace at the back wall was heaped with ashes and the ceiling and walls nearby had been blackened by smoke. Someone had lit a big fire that'd not ventilated well. Maybe they'd thrown on too much? The ashes had lumps that made me wonder if all of it had burned. Pale things, metallic objects too, poked above the general heap of blackness and my heart did an excited pitter pat. That might've been done at the last minute. I mean, who fired up this sort of rubbish and let it smother their house in smoke?

To me, little curiosity cat, this was like a Christmas present. I might find out stuff Wolfe would never say. Though I knelt before the fireplace for a closer look, I didn't touch. I grinned. Check out the rest then come back to this.

Another door, opposite where I'd entered, led into a bedroom. Double bed – a perfectly made bed that had been turned gray by the years and when I plonked my ass on it the dust billowed up.

Both in here and the library room, there were still-shuttered windows. Apart from a collapsed cupboard, there was a bedside table with three drawers. I pulled one out slowly, praying it wasn't made of the same inferior materials as the cupboard.

Inside was a gun. A big, fat revolver. If I picked it up, it didn't mean I'd have to use it on him. That was my first thought, and it rang in my head like a bell.

Don't do anything I wouldn't like. Those words resonated. He'd said them *days* ago.

I was pretty certain he'd pick up a gun, I told myself, very firmly, hammering in that logic.

Slowly, I reached out and wrapped my fingers around the body of the gun. Dust had sifted in and clung to oil on the surface that'd since turned stiff with all the material clogging it. I could wipe it away with a fingertip to show the metal beneath was clear of rust.

Was it loaded?

I blinked and thought that through. I didn't actually know how to shoot or use a gun. Fuck me though, wish I'd learned.

Hand shaking because of his words, I carried the gun out of the room and placed it on the floor beside the fireplace. Give myself some time and I might convince my brain to look at the weapon without shutting down.

I left the flashlight on but set it on the floor too, so it lit up the fireplace.

I couldn't shoot him, could I? I'd freeze up. The thing lay there, all fat and useless.

My sigh was long. No. I couldn't. Not physically, not morally. It didn't sit right. Maybe if he went to do something nasty...like beating my ass and back until I screamed?

Maybe?

Or not.

My parents could end up in prison if I couldn't see a way out of this. If I shot him...there went my leverage with the Russians too.

My bottom lip turned down and I screwed up my nose, as I tried to wrestle with all the permutations.

I was so messed up.

The fireplace poker lay near my knee. Rust dropped away and stained my hand when I picked it up. I broke down the long, solidified mass of ashes and burned papers, looking for anything left intact enough to identify. The air filled with motes of ash and I sneezed a few times then kept looking.

There was a charred journal and a slim, silver container that might've been an antique cigarette case, though the heat had melted the fine catch and the hinges. To get it open, I'd need to use a knife in the seam.

I found a dusty cloth on one of two small tables and wiped the case and what was left of the book. Half the pages were a mess of black and the rest were stuck together. Then I sifted through some of the rubbish beneath the center of the ashes. I wasn't plunging my hands in there, so I inserted the poker then dragged it back. The fifth time, a small object came with it.

I held it square in the light, rotated it. Mostly black but...

As a nurse, I knew in a half second, I'd found a small bone. Finger sized, in fact. My heart ticked over as my eyes refused to believe what I thought I held. Though crushed at one end, this seemed to be a finger bone. I scratched away ash and polished the surface, and underneath was paleness. Light in weight and the shape of it was a dead giveaway. Bone, for sure.

Why was there a part of a finger from a human in this fireplace?

Ancient history, but fascinating.

I slipped the bone into my shorts pocket, grabbed the book and the case, then rose to my feet. The stone had dug into me and my knees ached, but a question overrode the discomfort.

Should I ask Wolfe about this when he returned? Some terrible accident might've occurred in the past. He might not have been here though, or heard of it. No crime that came to the attention of the police, where someone lost a finger, would leave the remains of the finger here. Even if not a crime, you just wouldn't do it, surely? It had to be unknown, a secret.

I'd still ask him.

The book, though, and the case? I wanted to hide those. I went to and fro on that. They could be innocent things, so it'd be perfectly okay to put them away somewhere. And the gun? My coerced conscience prompted. Would Wolfe be okay with me hiding *that*?

Crap. I swallowed. No. I couldn't logic away that one.

I walked back out to the kitchen and tucked the book and the case into a bottom drawer at the counter, the lowest one of four drawers and next to the floor. I shut it with my foot then weighed the gun in my hand. The temptation was strong and still I couldn't make myself hide it.

The front door banged open and Wolfe strode in – wild look in his eyes, a pack dangling from one fist, the keys from the car jangling in the other.

That distant rumbling my mind had barely noticed, had been the SUV returning.

"What is that?"

Panicked already, I looked at the revolver then at him. I thrust it at him, trigger guard presented first. "I found it. I was going to give it to you. I swear. Here." Again, I gestured with the gun.

Pack and keys were dropped at his feet, then he took one long stride and engulfed my gun-holding hand with his.

The gun was wrenched from my hand and tossed backward, skidding on stone.

Not good gun safety.

Flustered, I backed up. The drug must be dangerously low in his blood.

"I'll get you some food."

"You don't touch that gun again."

"I won't." My throat tightened.

"Good. First, you. *Then* food."

Oh fuck.

"Me? I mean –"

His hand arrived at my throat then slowly clamped in. "You."

The thrill of recognition of his beast-man state was disconcerting. I managed to swallow.

I should protest some more.

Should.

But he spun me around, yanked down my shorts, and tore off the snap fastener, sending it rattling across the floor.

My only thought as he pushed aside my underwear, stuck himself inside me, and made my eyes glaze – *I have no way to sew that back on.*

"You don't." He fucked me for a few strokes, lifting me off my toes. "Touch gun."

Cheek sliding on the dusty countertop, I barely understood his words.

"Yes?"

He wanted an answer? I grappled uselessly with the timber under

99

my face, rousing myself from the fog of desire. At the increased force of his last ram up inside, his cock had thickened, pulsed. "Fuck," I whispered, eyelids flicking open and shut. "I...yes."

"No touch?"

God, that deep growl at my neck and the painful scrape of his stubble.

I went up on tip toes, begging for more but he stayed deep and still. "Yes! No touch."

"Good." His chuckle made me open my eyes and try to shift to look back at him. He grabbed a big chunk of my hair and forced my cheek back down on the countertop. "Your cunt tries to suck me in?"

Eh. He was right. Stretched deliciously by cock, it was dilating then clamping down in that reflexive response.

"You want me to fuck you, hey?"

That question had to be rhetorical, besides...besides, he felt so good. I only grunted, waited.

"No. You come outside."

Cursing quietly, I felt him withdraw, leaving me empty and needy. I straightened then twisted. My hands were still propped on the counter – guess I was hoping he'd change his mind, whatever mind Mister Primitive had left at this moment.

Outside? Why there? The tablets were in the car inside my handbag, in the hidden zip pocket, and difficult to get to.

What did he mean to do? Unease travelled through me, cold and worming, making my nipples hard.

"Off." Then he pulled my sweater over my head.

With my T-shirt and sweater pulled off and dropped to the floor, he moved to grab my hand and tow me out the door, but I realized there had never been a command. Sometimes I felt the waning of his power, or just the absence, and this was one of those times. I skipped away, both appalled at my action and excited.

His lip raised in a snarl and around his eyes wrinkled as anger spread.

It was an *oops* moment that made my heart kick into panic time – shuddering then knocking out hammer beats.

Run? Stay to let god knew what happen? I feared. I ran. In this small room I ducked away then managed to flee out the door, almost going under his arm, feeling the scrape of his nails on my skin.

I pelted outside, underwear clad only, and found the SUV sitting there, purring, engine still going, *and the driver's door open.* He'd forgotten, or meant to back it around to unload, I didn't care.

I could leave.

Fuck. It made no sense in some ways. I knew he was close behind but I reasoned in my panic that I could pile in the driver's side and once I locked the door, I could go, just *go.*

Seconds before I'd been dying for him to fuck me. That wasn't sane.

None of this was.

I ran, I reached the car and leaped in, with him pounding along behind me, silent. No commands. He must know they weren't working.

The door. I scrabbled, shifting my ass, and found the handle, hooked my hand in, and slammed the door shut, locked it. The quiet in here was astounding. I was under the sea, floundering, flailing, my heartbeat winding down, my ears hurting from the silence, and there was the stare of the man leaning over the hood, hands planted wide, and he was only a yard away. Then it was inches away, just across the glass – his blue eyes potent and piercing, nailing me to the seat. My lips parted, relaxing. My mind filled with fuzziness.

He knew my buttons.

"Out." The muffled word bounced about then seated in my mind. *Click.* Solid as stone.

I opened the door and slipped from the seat, only to be observed until I went to my knees, trembling.

Wolfe. This was my god, for this day at least.

"You don't run. You don't touch guns. You're mine and you *stay.*" The words were ground out then he turned back to the house.

He walked inside then around the outside, searching maybe. Stunned to within an inch of total blankness, I waited, my lower lip pinched in teeth. He emerged with a rusted chain over his shoulder and took a loop of rope from the back of the SUV before he returned to me.

His hand settled on my neck, half-circled the front, and he dragged me backward toward one of the few large white pines growing near the cabin.

Roughly, he surrounded my neck with the inch-wide chain, using rope to join one end to the rest of the chain and forming a collar.

The rope he took to the tree trunk, wrapping it around and tying it in place. I could feel the weight of the excess chain pulling and rust smeared my palms when I picked up the trailing end.

"Leave it be."

Blinking, I dropped it and he *tsked* at the rust on my hands then went to one knee. Wolfe pulled me forward until I had to go to hands and knees or end up face first in the grass. I felt him unclasp my bra and he sat me up to slide it down my arms. The sun was out in force but the mountain coolness drew goosebumps along my arms and shriveled my nipples to perky buttons.

"Show hands."

Kneeling pertly, I held out my hands, palm up. They were covered with dirt and grass, as well as rust.

"Dirty. Such a dirty, naughty girl."

His statement oozed a combination of menace and amusement and was said while he wiped off most of the dirt using my bra as a rag.

"Mmm," was my one audible comment.

The hard, grinding kiss he next bestowed on me rattled me even more.

Lust and control were imbued in Wolfe's every word and movement, in the way he handled me, even in how he took over my thoughts and actions. I had little chance to think.

When he bent me backward using a grip on my jaw, with my legs still in the kneeling position, I had to prop myself on my arms.

"Open." He slapped my thighs until I spread them. Then I swallowed, pulse already leaping, mind already centered, as he rolled aside my flimsy underwear. They were already soaked from when he'd half-fucked me before. I strained forward as the thickness of two fingers scissored my entrance open and thrust inside, far enough in to make me groan. My clit swelled at the immense pleasure that simple act unleashed on me.

"I do what I like. Hmmm?" He shook my throat. "I chain you to tree. I fuck you. I not fuck you."

To speak, I first needed to swallow and rearrange my mind. Words. What the fuck were those when this man was inside me? "Yes." I opened my eyes and found his molten gaze upon me.

"Good. Stay there while I bite you."

My legs were doubled over, my feet felt crushed and locked

beneath me, and his hand on my throat kept me leaning backward as if a wind had blown me over.

Blinking became impossible. Pain was coming. Letting out tiny screams at each new bite, I felt him leave teeth marks all up and down my thighs. The last was above my clit, barely a half-inch above. His fingers had kept on fucking me. As the last bite continued and the force increased, I held my breath for at most another second before I screamed a string of frantic curses.

He released my skin and I stopped screaming.

Above my gasping, all I could hear were the wet sounds coming from where he penetrated me with his fingers. When he licked me that one swipe of tongue across clit slammed me into a thigh-trembling state, seconds from coming.

Then he released me, let me be, and stood.

I heard the metallic rasp of a zipper. My legs and arms shook from the nearness of a climax almost, but not quite, extracted.

Weak, I was such a weak person. Tears trailed down the sides of my face.

A moment later, I was pinned with my back to the tree while he opened my mouth with his thumbs and fucked it. Confusion built and spread, erasing thought while he invaded my mouth, scraping past teeth and tongue. When he came, his cum spilled from my mouth. I could barely recall how to close it as I gulped for air.

"You want to come too?" he whispered, his palm pressing on my pussy. "Let me kiss that dirty mouth then tell me."

Kissing stripped the last of my thoughts away. I'm sure I sat there unspeaking for a long time before he awoke me with a light slap.

"You want to come, Kiara?"

I coughed and licked my lips, tasting him. Cleaning off the rest of the residue my tongue could reach gave me some respite, some quiet time. I knew what I wanted to say, but what did he expect?

"Mmm? I do?"

"I might let you. Later." Then he strode away, leaving me sprawled against the tree.

Disappointment almost made me plead.

I closed my eyes, thought about closing my legs but didn't bother.

Recovery, resetting my brain, must've taken a while.

The world shouldn't revolve around fucking.

If only the ache between my legs would go away.

When next I saw Wolfe, he was eating a leg of roast chicken, ripping flesh off bone. Where that had come from I didn't know. I grieved that he wasn't eating any Keppra. If I wasn't loose, how could I medicate him? My own stomach rumbled and I wondered if it were close to lunchtime already.

I had to get free.

Soon.

Soon never arrived.

After that, he kept coming back and half-fucking me, getting me all tuned in and turned on for climaxing before leaving me unfulfilled. The throb in my pussy intensified to a maddening amount, until I wondered why I hadn't come when he'd done so much.

The last time, when he stopped and walked away, I found myself rocking in place. Awful.

He could give and he could take away.

After he fucked me and came, twice, I awakened to myself writhing on the ground, making strange, pitiful sounds. Levering myself off the ground took much of the last of my strength. On hands and knees, through a fringe of sweat-soaked hair, I eyed the SUV where he'd parked it, three yards away.

I'd had no water or food, though I was under shade, and dusk was coming. If he left me out here overnight, anything might happen, even death. It wasn't that cold, if you had clothes on, but dehydrated and exhausted?

Maybe I could dig a hole in the earth like a husky in snow?

Or, better, cut him open, like Luke Skywalker did that hairy tauntaun creature, and use him as cave.

If only.

I wouldn't though. I needed him.

Pouting, I lay down and curled into a ball, shivering. Frustrating, so frustrating.

When I awoke, he was fucking me again, from behind and he'd pulled me onto hands and knees. I was sticky and dirty but that didn't worry him. This time, the tension had me crying out with each thrust. The unfulfilled craving compelled me to bite when he slapped his hand over my mouth. Rocked forward, my body caving so that only my ass was raised, dirt and grass filled my mouth as he crammed himself in so far up inside that I ceased to breathe, to think. I'm sure my heart stilled as an orgasm stormed through me, shook me, and spat me out a desultory, drooling mess.

Trembling, I clutched the earth, aware that he was biting me. Hot pain lanced into my shoulder as he spilled inside me.

The rumble of secondary pleasure, from him to me, blew away my knowledge of existence.

I tumbled.

My brain short-circuited.

I was getting used to this. I found myself gathering up the threads I'd lost and surfacing, bobbing slowly. Wolfe was still here, still inside, licking blood off my shoulder. Knew it was blood. The hurt was sharp and made me wince with every rasp of his tongue. Though I wriggled, he held me to him.

Night-time had flung a cascade of stars across the sky. How long had we lain here? Had I lost track of time completely?

If I didn't get some drug into him, if this kept up...

But I couldn't go anywhere. Not without permission.

Fuck. I ground my forehead on the grass.

There must be a way.

"Hungry?" I tempted him, this man who'd regressed so far that words might soon lose significance for him.

He grunted and licked me again.

"I'll get us food? Food?"

The wait to see if he could understand was agonizing. If I lost this opportunity there might be no other.

Only a grunt came back...but it'd sounded like an affirmative. I chose to believe that, hanging onto my interpretation as I searched for where he'd tied the chain together. The knot was tight but I picked at it. My fingers wore away from the roughness of the hemp. Several minutes later, I was free. I crept to my knees, whispering again, *food*, then standing, stumbling.

His eyes were closed. Though my legs shook, and my knees gave way every few steps, I made it to the SUV. My hand didn't seem mine. Numb and swaying in place, I searched blindly beneath the passenger seat and found my bag. The remains of the roast chicken lay on the ground nearby, shredded, picked mostly clean, and likely to give me food poisoning. Though I hesitated, I didn't eat any. I picked up a handful of chicken pieces to mix with the powdered pill.

If it was too nasty tasting? What then? I bit back a sob and swept away my bedraggled hair. This had to work.

Somehow I made it back to him, fed him the tablet and chicken directly, made him eat it, though pieces fell to the ground. He grabbed me after that and wouldn't let go. Tears sent me back toward sleep. I was warmer, cradled in his arms, though my mouth was dry as bone and my stomach empty. It would do. Would have to.

I had nothing else...nothing.

CHAPTER 18

Kiara

Waking was a painful process as every movement reminded me of various hurts. Between my legs was sore. As if that were a surprise. My left shoulder, just below the angle of my neck was the worst. Grunting, I struggled upright onto my elbow, finding myself on a mattress with a sleeping bag under me. And over me. The light pouring in the window made squinting necessary.

This was the bedroom. Bright now, but the same place – collapsed cupboard, the set of drawers near my elbow, and the door to the library room was open. Then the bed shifted and I gasped and looked over my shoulder. Wolfe was here, behind me, sitting on the other side of the bed.

His neat, if crinkled, mauve shirt, tidy and tied back hair, and the gentleness in his eyes convinced me *he* was back. Not the beast, thank god. The one with smarts and some common sense. The one who didn't try to kill me by fucking me to death.

"Here." He offered a bottle and I took it and gulped down some water.

My lips were cracked and the feel of water going down my throat would've rivalled ambrosia from the gods.

I'd thought him my god. When was that, yesterday? I swallowed more water, then more again, and all he did was watch, wearing a kindly if guarded smile with his big hands on his lap.

Even now, after everything, the sway of his dark locks across his face and the strength in those corded neck muscles moved me. Which was so impossibly stupid.

"I cleaned you up, put some underwear on you. Gave you water too, when you'd take it."

I'd been exhausted, but it surprised me I'd slept through, or forgotten, all that. I tested the air, my mind, found his commanding aura weak though present. Speaking seemed dangerous, like it'd break the spell.

That might've been nonsense if not for the hint of something deeper and crueler that surfaced in a flash when the top of the sleeping bag slipped and revealed my breasts...well, a pink bra really.

Then Mister Nice seemed to settle over him. It'd been his eyes that'd showed mean.

"Thanks," I ventured. Did he not recall what he'd done?

Wolfe nodded, stood, and headed for the doorway. "I put a bandaid on your neck."

I raised my hand and touched it. An amateur effort with two thin dressings. It'd be the devil to peel those off the punctures if, as I suspected, he'd stuck them to the wound.

Saying thanks for that would be ridiculous. It was a bite mark. His bite mark. I vaguely recalled him sinking his teeth into me and the blood. The swelling and tenderness made me wonder about infection. Mouths had nasty bacteria.

However, gold star award for me, the drug had worked on Wolfe. Gingerly, I sat up, clutching the sleeping bag to my chest.

"There's breakfast. I brought a generator back, meat, vegetables. I can't run it all day but the little fridge will keep cold a while."

WTF. He brought what? "And no one noticed you stealing all that?"

"Taking it?" Hand on the door frame, he stopped and glanced back. His mouth twisted. "Yes, they did, but they won't tell."

I bit back a question about whether he'd fucked them too. A. I didn't really want to know. B. I hoped his dick dropped off if he had. C. Yes. I was jealous. And D? It was so illogical I wasn't going there.

Sighing, I slid to my feet. "I'll be out soon."

Breakfast. I could smell bacon. Holy mother of dragons. Bacon!

Without another word, he exited. Not a single, *sorry I fucked you and nearly killed you with exposure, exhaustion, and dehydration.* What did I expect? Sorry was for couples who truly cared about each other. To

Wolfe I was just a sex object.

I found denim shorts and a sweater, dressed, and followed him out through the musty library. A few of the books looked to have been picked up and the pile of ashes had been removed from the fireplace. The man had been tidying up.

When I saw the plateful of bacon, eggs, and hash browns at the kitchen table, I was a goner. My stomach would worship him at least.

I sat on the chair provided and tucked in with knife and fork. Wolfe leaned back in his chair with a satisfied air, as if seeing me eating gave him pleasure. He hadn't said sorry, but maybe I could get him to let me be the orchestrator of his food, and so give him the drug more precisely. The last attempt had failed.

"You know you nearly killed me?" I said softly. My last morsel of food stuck halfway down my throat while I stewed on his reply.

He grunted.

That was...encouraging.

Smoke drifted in through the door and I gathered he'd cooked outside over a fire. If the oven could be used, we could have proper hot meals. I snorted. So mundane.

"You, um, need to let me prepare your meals. It'll help you, and me." Calculating fast, I figured I only had a month's worth of pills left.

After that, who was I kidding? How could I plan that far? I'd almost died. This...I looked again out the fully open window, it must be past midday. All that time had gone past. How much had he remembered?

"You know you did something bad..." *To me.*

The gargantuan bulk of him, his thick fingers and heavy hands, the way his hair hid his eyes at times and he peered out...he might've been a troll dug up from the earth. An orc from some *The Lord of the Rings* story, except somewhat handsomer, and minus tusks.

And then I knew, I just *knew*, that he recalled little.

If I squinted and forgot all his anatomy, that he breathed, I could see him as a storm, not an ill-natured creature. He was a force of nature, and who could blame the wind for where it blew?

Even if a lie, that way of seeing him let me talk to him without freezing up. Because I hated the irrational uncertainty, the danger that lurked. If he suddenly leaped up, I'd scream.

Still he was silent.

My heart knocked away, loud enough to make me doubt my bravery. *Shut up heart.*

"If it will help, sure, you can dole out the food."

Yesss. "Good." If I was careful, very careful, I could control him. "Thanks."

Another grunt.

The conversation was scintillating today.

Shit. I chilled. Was he shutting down? His next dose was needed, *now.*

"You should have something to eat, right away."

At his nod, relief surged. Getting there. Next, those glittery red shoes to click.

"There's boiled water outside if you want coffee?"

"Great." I needed to get the pills in a way that wasn't suspicious. "I use a sugar substitute. Is my handbag out there?"

"Yes. In the car."

I sauntered out, aware that he was watching me, or my ass, but I retrieved the pills and my bag, and I vowed to hide half of them in the kitchen from now on.

So weird to have long-term goals.

I should, as in *ASAP* type of should, bomb his brain out of existence with a double dose.

Except his get-out-of-jail statement – *don't do anything I wouldn't like,* stuck me into a loop. He wouldn't like me doing that...therefore I couldn't do it. I ground up the extra dose and had to tip it into the dirt because my traitorous hands wouldn't let me put it in the coffee. His coffee and his cheese sandwich ended up with a normal dose of Keppra instead.

When in the middle of sipping my coffee, the solution popped up. I had to see double dosing him as what he would want. How?

Maybe it was impossible and maybe not. I shouldn't give in.

Though stiff and sore, with bruises coming out everywhere, I helped him unload gear from the SUV and get the cabin in order. Via a long electrical cord he'd already connected the generator that he'd left outside, under cover, to the little fridge, which was in the kitchen. I swept out dust, threw out ancient cloths, picked up fallen things, and admired the running water in the sink.

He'd cleared the plumbing while I'd been in bed, asleep. It didn't look drinkable and probably had the corpses of a million bugs swimming in it, but it was water.

"We'd have to boil that to use it."

I nodded.

We.

I touched the bandaid on my neck. That word made us seem like some old married couple, and that was as far as could you get from the truth without catching a train.

* * * * *

That day hadn't been fruitful with regards to words exchanged. Though I hadn't been sure I wanted to talk to him much.

Today, though...

With all the cleaning and repairs, I followed him around like a new puppy at its master's heels. It led me to places I might not have ventured otherwise. Such as while he was on the roof, checking the roofing iron, I found where he'd dumped the ashes at the back of the cabin. The mess called to me, saying *poke me*. So, I did.

Lo and behold, I found more blackened bones. Small ones. Crushed ones. Maybe ones that'd been chewed on. It made sense if you thought of someone eating the cooked tail of some animal. Only...who did that? Unless you were very hungry.

And still, the resemblance to human bones worried me, absorbed me, made me store them in my jeans pocket in the hope of googling or textbooking again one day. I just needed someone who knew bones intimately.

One of my quirks. This would bug me forever.

Or until Wolfe climbed down and took my hand, and drew me away. Holding hands was troublesome. I wanted his touch, *craved* it severely, and I detested it.

Like the touch of a new lover, he enlivened me every, single time we made skin contact.

Sometimes I shut my eyes to experience that reverberating tingle more intensely.

Junkie. I was a touch junkie.

Didn't matter what he did to me.

He could probably cut holes in me, fuck them, stitch them up, and still I'd crawl back and beg. That thought made me shudder.

I bit my lip to camouflage my dismay.

What was I going to do?

But I let him lead me onward.

We walked through scrubby bushes and rocks, then through a small concave field, to where a slope overlooked a stream. Fifty yards below a carpet of nodding blue flowers, water gurgled over rocks sending up tiny flashes of sunlight.

The height and the lack of trees meant the wind took full advantage and blew in gusts at times, but I'd suffer that just for the view, for the illusion of freedom. My blue dress flapped against my legs and I clutched the side to hold it still.

My face felt odd, then I smiled, and it was as if it'd cracked. Surely, it was the first time I'd smiled for days. "This is beautiful."

Wolfe had laid out the picnic rug he'd brought – a grotesque, tartan-red thing. "Sit."

I eyed the rug then lowered myself, folding my legs into a lotus position and tucking the dress into my lap. A second later, he sat behind me, enclosing me in the V of his legs.

Though I wasn't sure why we were here, I guessed he wanted to talk. If just the view, he could've come by himself...unless he wanted to share it with me? I didn't want to start the talking. I barely wanted to hear what he might say.

The anxiety of having him sit behind me made me jump when he stroked a finger across the bandage. I'd redone the dressing as well as I could without a mirror. Strange, but it seemed cleaner and better today than yesterday. Infection had seemed a given.

"I did this?"

Fuck, man. You don't even remember this? I compressed my lips. "Yes."

And still no sorry came.

I had a question: *What do you remember?* The sentence stuck and wouldn't come out, no matter how many times I went to say it.

The silence stretched and broke down into the sigh of trees, and the rustle of a thousand grass heads and flower blooms rubbing against each other, lasciviously, under the sun.

"Lie back," he said.

I didn't protest. What would be the point? I lay back until my head rested on his chest, under his chin and his arms wrapped about me, as if he meant to protect me.

Laughable, but I was drunk-drowsy on the fumes of his nearby existence. He affected me without question, without permission, without thinking.

For once, I don't think he meant to.

By then I was waiting to be molested.

"Your family..."

"Huh?" I roused.

"You said they would suffer if you didn't do as your superiors told you to."

The real world intruded.

"Yes. True."

Beneath my ear, I counted several hypnotic heartbeats – his.

"Why?"

"Because, my stepfather did something that is legally treason. Because they wanted to get me to agree to spying, or..." I waved my hand. "Whatever they decided needed doing."

"Kidnapping."

"Yes." I frowned. And that hadn't turned out so well. I wondered where they'd ended up, and what they thought. "God!" I almost sat up straight but he tightened his hold.

"What?"

"If they think I've deliberately disobeyed... They might've already locked away my stepfather, or executed him."

"Not if they know I abducted you."

"Why would they see it that way?"

"You said they were watching us. That means they would've seen what I did to you in the alley."

"Oh." True. My mind ticked over. They must know of his powers. The longer I was with him, the more obvious that seemed. They'd know I'd had no choice.

I hadn't thought this through for days. I'd simply lost track of the world out there. Sobering.

And here he was helping me out, reassuring me even? Was this what the drug did at the dose I'd given today? Made him into a reasonable person?

If so...

"Maybe you should let me go?"

"No."

Hmmm. I was all alone in this, but at least the only person who could get hurt was me.

"How much do you remember?" I blurted that out, finally.

"Of what happened two days ago?"

"Yes."

"Enough. You?"

"That wasn't a trick question," I said, annoyed.

"I remember fucking you." He squeezed his arms in. "I remember it felt good. I remember you crying out and shaking when you came."

I'd wanted remorse, instead I got...a happy recitation. I lowered my head, wondering. If he had a conscience, now was the best chance I'd had to dig it out of his soul.

"Do you remember how ill I was?"

"Yes."

And aren't you sorry? I would never ask him that. He'd say it by his own volition, or he wouldn't.

"Have you ever felt that deeply before, Kiara? Ever lived that close to the edge? Ever soared so close to the sun that your feathers might melt?"

His hands crept beneath my dress. Warm hands on my cold thighs, and I expected to be ravished at any moment. Instead, he leaned around and looked me in the eyes.

"Have you?"

Did I climax until my toes might've melted? Yes. I wasn't sure about feathers. And I wasn't agreeing with him even with his fingers inches from my pussy.

"I've never been that close to dying, no." I switched topics. "Why are you here, Wolfe?"

I didn't get an immediate answer, though I could tell from the movement of his chest that he was thinking.

Birds flew past, scolding each other, and the air lost another degree. We should be heading back. The generator only had so much fuel and running it for lights was foolish.

"I'm here to find out who I am. I think Magnus has the answer. Something here calls me, whispers in my ear.

"What does it say?"

"Nothing plain yet. I have a ton of questions, though. Why do the Russians want me? How did I get this power? Who am I, is at the bottom of the pile. What about you? What do you want?"

Some of those questions were mine too.

His fingers were moving, treadling into my flesh, like a man tapping and considering his next move.

I held my breath. Once again I betrayed myself. I was imagining his fingers piercing me.

And blood coming out, and more blood, a red tide. Fuck. Begone nightmare vision.

"I want..." I gulped and went for it. "Freedom."

"But what sort?" He withdrew his hands and rearranged my dress. "Who is ever free? When we think we are, we're mostly running on treadmills. Everyone dances to someone else's tune. The best? When you make that tune yours, because that makes you *live*."

Then he kissed my neck and said his last words to me as if they were something he'd lifted from a statue, an inscription of truth.

"We're never free. We can only dare to run the line between destruction and glory."

Goosebumps were still shivering across my skin when he rose to his feet.

Confused and a little dazed, I looked up at him. Was that it?

He offered me his hand and I took it.

Destruction or glory? A white picket fence and 2.5 children wasn't exactly my dream, but there had to be something else in between?

On the way back, he collected flowers and twisted the stems together until he had a circlet.

He placed it on my head as if it were some beautiful crown, adjusting my hair so it stayed on. Funny, it really affected me, having him this friendly.

I shot him a coy look then asked my big question, again. "When are you letting me go?"

"Never."

Dang. Same answer, same nonchalance in the reply, but it didn't fill me with fear as I should. Like this, I could handle Wolfe.

CHAPTER 19

Kiara

When I could do it without being seen, I cleaned those bones until they were white. I kept them in my pocket as some sort of talisman. Maybe they'd help me think. When I got him to say sorry, that'd mean he regretted what he'd done, which'd mean he agreed he shouldn't do that to me again...

Which would mean I would be fine with giving him a huge dose of Keppra until he could barely walk, let alone *think*. Because that would stop him doing things to me.

Then I could escape. Correct?

Theoretically. It gave me an aim.

But he never said sorry. Every time he sneaked down to town, he did however remind me: *Don't do anything I wouldn't like.*

Scared to alter it, I kept the dose as constant as I could, and I gave him pre-dosed food to take with him, just in case he was stuck down there.

I had a few close calls where I thought he'd seen me adding the drug to his food and it left me anxious. I was going to run out eventually. He was the only person who could get more. When I was down to four doses, I'd tell him. That gave me time to talk and think, to connive, to follow up clues about Magnus. All the dusty empty photo frames intrigued me.

And the way Wolfe acted while on this dose intrigued me too.

He fixed up things at a steady pace. The tank water running into the sink was clean looking, though we still boiled it. The roof was clear of debris. The insides of the cabin were getting cleaner, more ordered, less dusty, though that was more my doing.

We had a double quilt on the bed with frickin' cherries on it!

Little, red cherries. It looked so cute I wondered when the matching curtains would turn up. Of course laundry was a task and a half. A bear wandered across the front yard one day, disappeared, and I never saw it again. The countryside sort of meandered into my life when it felt like it.

Next thing, we'd have pots of bright-colored geraniums on the window sill and neighbors coming in to have a beer. As if we had any neighbors. When all the shutters were open, on the sunny days, the cabin was a place to warm your soul.

And with me was the man least likely to win daddy-of-the-year award, or husband.

If he turned bad again...

I tended to some cuts on his hands once, though they were likely to heal no matter what I did. Still, blood spotting the earth as he walked toward me had made my caring heart go *lub dub dub*. Treating his wounds made me feel useful.

He'd been bringing me flowers. Chocolates from the town, once. *Lindt* chocs. *OMG*.

I sat in the sun after that, eating them with him, drinking coffee, turning this all over. I mustn't become complacent.

I couldn't find anything in the cabin that told me much about its previous inhabitant. Wolfe seemed calmer, but otherwise his daily walks alone yielded no revelations – or none he told me about.

Then one day, and I had no idea anymore what day of the week it was, Wolfe brought the gun to me and he told me: "I'm going to teach you to shoot."

Fear entered me at the same moment he took me by the hand. Was there some hidden reason? He was giving me the gun he'd forbidden me to touch.

Wolfe led me across that little hollow field to the place above the creek. Our feet crunched the grass underfoot, bees buzzed, the birds made their melodious sounds, and I feared.

Guns were not something I'd ever like. They killed. They were made for killing people, worst of all. You didn't hunt duck with a revolver.

I wore jeans and a tank top. It'd rained yesterday, like it did half the time here, but today was warm enough to get a tan. So normal.

"Here." Wolfe showed me the gun. "Put out your hand. I'll show you how to clean it, strip it, another time. Hand?"

I couldn't raise my arm and ended up giving him a quizzical look, half embarrassment, half scared. He'd told me never to touch it.

From the twisting lines on his face, he hadn't figured it out. Then his face cleared. "Oh. You can do this, Kiara. I give you permission to shoot the gun."

At that, I found I could take it from him.

"This is the safety. You turn it off like this. Or on. Then raise it and use the sights...keep your wrist..."

I listened, feeling distant. Why didn't he expect me to shoot him? Had he been that sure of me, or was he not thinking things through?

The rest of the lesson went in a blur, though I did what he asked and shot at some cans he'd set up. Since we were on a slope, it wasn't simple. There was elevation to consider, and wind, and possibly the price of eggs in China. I hit a few targets and he took the revolver back to reload it.

"Why are you doing this?" God damn, I'd been dying to ask.

"Because..." He looked up from his task. "I want you to be safe."

From who?

"People might come here while I'm gone. You know?"

Ohhh. Safe, safe. Not...so that I could shoot him if he went nuts again.

He hadn't made a move on me in ages. Crazily, as seemed often the case when it involved Wolfe, I kind of missed sex with him. And that I couldn't remember us ever having what I'd call normal sex? Yup, scary.

I had the dose down to an exactitude now. He never varied in behavior. I'd ventured a smaller dose TID not BID. For some reason, it worked well. His system might metabolize the drug faster than most?

And right when I was thinking through all that, and Wolfe was readying the gun, from behind him something rustled straight toward us through the grass, burrowing and making this rasping sound. Then that something barreled into Wolfe's legs.

It went up on its hind legs and scratched at his jeans.

The something was small and rotund, black and white, with cute poppy eyes and a tongue as long as an unrolled rug. It leaped about barking and scratching some more, then it ran in circles about us both, weaving through our legs.

"A dog?" Wolfe said, incredulously.

"A Boston Terrier?" I added, just as astounded.

"Where in hell did you come from?"

We both looked around but no one else could be seen or heard.

Wolfe checked the gun's safety then holstered it and went to one knee. Grinning at the creature's antics, I went to my knees also.

From the way she behaved, as we both patted her, pats were in short supply.

"You think its owner's around?"

"Don't know." Wolfe put both hands on it and found a weathered collar. "No tag. No phone number. Maybe a camper lost her. She reminds me of a dog I once had..."

"Oh?"

"Her name was Lily. We'll keep this girl until her owner shows up. *You* can be Lily 2." Then he held my gaze, firmer than he had for many days, his eyes narrowing. "If anyone comes and I'm here, call me. If I'm not..."

"Don't do anything I wouldn't like," I recited.

"Yes. That. And be safe."

"You going to leave me the gun?" *Haha.* I raised a brow and put hand to hip, challenging him.

"I will."

Wow.

At that Lily 2 bounced onto his lap then jumped again to lick his mouth. The spluttering commenced and I almost fell over laughing – had to prop myself off the ground with my arm. Wolfe, grinning, gave me a shove and I toppled over backward into the grass.

It wasn't meant to happen, obviously...I was beginning to think his libido was zero on this dose, but...he leaned over me, with his arms to either side, and he crawled up my body.

The dog must've been puzzled or curious, or exhausted, as she flopped down and watched.

I hadn't had this man being sexually attentive for ages, and yet, despite everything, he revved me up in one second flat – as soon as his groin pressed onto me. Soon as he observed my mouth when I licked my bottom lip...when he put a finger to the neckline of my shirt and traced it from my shoulder, tickling me, making me breathless, all the way to my cleavage.

Wolfe had ravaged me, tied me to a tree, and fucked me senseless, and here I was urging him onward with my hand on his jaw and the other to his shirt.

Buttons, why did he have buttons?

From the way he tugged my jeans button loose, he had the same problem.

I laughed as he kissed me and helped him shrug me out of my shirt and wriggle my jeans past my butt, then further. Eventually they were off entirely and we'd exchanged hot kisses, warm sighs, some curious gazes as we admired each other's bodies. I shuddered when he shifted between my legs and moaned as he entered me.

He didn't stay inside me after a few thrusts. He was a thoughtful lover.

When he came, I guess it was a minute after he'd brought me to orgasm too, with his fingers and mouth on my pussy. I lay there afterward, with the dog a yard away snoring, and when the word *nice* came into my head I realized how apt that was. The lovemaking had been nice and almost satisfying.

Almost.

I snuggled deeper into his arms and wondered if the grass would leave me itchy. At least we had that creek to wash in, though it'd be freezing.

Nice.

Dammit. I was feeling disappointed and I knew why, couldn't ignore my own reasons.

I expected more from Wolfe. I'd wanted him to fuck me like there was no tomorrow, riding that line between destruction and glory, leaving a burning line on the world you could see from the heavens. Something like that. I twitched my mouth. I was being silly.

But as I felt him plant a kiss on my nape and stroke my hair, my dismay mingled with a ridiculous amount of sorrow.

I guess that's when I made a little jump and fell into some surreal other world, because the thought I'd just had run through my head couldn't have been mine.

What if...what if I lowered the dose just a bit, to get him...less tame?

It was something to muse over. No hurry.

Another thought sidled in too. Holding the gun had jarred a memory into being. Being told not to touch it had left a scar, somehow, and had obscured something that I really should've followed up on. The charred journal and the cigarette case were waiting for me.

CHAPTER 20

Kiara

No one had come looking for the dog. When Wolfe went out on his solitary walk, she trotted along beside him until he scooped her up. Bostons weren't made for jogging, exercising, or anything that involved breathing hard. He'd be doing a lot of carrying. I levered myself away from the kitchen door jamb and made a beeline for that drawer that held the journal.

With butter knife in hand, I settled on the floor, with a folded rug under me to cushion my butt. Wolfe would be a fair while, and I knew the noises to listen for now. It was unlikely he'd surprise me. Besides, I wasn't doing anything wrong.

The front of the book was a list of stuff someone had bought, maybe? Prices, dates, etcetera. Only toward the end did it turn into a diary of sorts. A short one, with the pages burned in half.

I read page after page about this Magnus waffling on about how fantastic some woman was, then it degenerated into strange statements, one per page, then it stopped with the oddest of them all, and I sat back.

I did something terrible.

I'm sorry Amelia.

That was it.

Had he done something terrible to her? Or was this him apologizing to her for doing that terrible thing?

No way to tell. Maybe I had her fingers in my pocket. Now that'd be really strange and gruesome.

He obviously didn't live here anymore. Wolfe wasn't the least concerned his pal would turn up.

The cigarette case was next. I stood and checked out the window. It'd not taken more than twenty minutes to slice open the burnt edges, sweep the ashes from the pages with my fingers, and read Magnus's careful handwriting. I had time.

The case was thin and thoroughly distorted at the seam and hinges. When wriggling in the butter knife only bent the knife edge, I found a heavier knife. Then I stared at it, turned it over. It was some sort of hunting knife Wolfe had left on the counter top.

He was so sure of me that he left lethal things lying about. Or he didn't care if I tried. If so, he was fatalistic. It might also be a test.

I shook my head and set to trying to lever open the case. Finally, it cracked. A small piece of hinge flew across the floor. I put down the knife and bent the case open all the way. Inside was more paper, only these were photos. The heat from the fire had destroyed some of them, or left only tattered and shriveled things that might've been pictures of UFOs for all I could tell. A few from the center of the pile were mostly intact.

Eleven recognizable photos in all.

I laid them in a row on the floor, then picked up each one and scrutinized it, front and back. A few had a dates or names on the back. One photo was of someone called Amelia. Her name on the back was inside a sketched heart and written in what seemed to be Magnus's hand.

She was a pretty redhead, with short hair and a wide smile of the sort that looked model girl. Happy though. Magnus couldn't have been too awful. Another photo had birthday party written on the back. The front showed a table with several people sitting at it. Two men had their arms around their girlfriends or wives.

The other woman, by herself, was her. Amelia.

She was smiling at the camera, in an intimate way. She held a wine glass and hanging from her wrist was a pretty gold-and-amethyst bracelet. I adored that purple gemstone. A third of the photo was gone. The burned edge showed only part of the chair beside her and on it was probably a small dog. I could see the hind leg. Black, like Lily? Was this Wolfe's previous dog? If a friend of Magnus, he might've been there.

"Hmmm."

Being Detective Kiara was the most fun I'd had for *days*. Wolfe was once again in eunuch mode.

Another four, undamaged photos: a group of different people; a view of this cabin from the outside; a photo looking down the hallway where Amelia posed in a black catsuit. The catsuit had a chunky zip that ran all the way down between her legs and her breasts were bared. The photo was floodlit, somehow, from above. The last photo was a close-up of the bracelet. Perhaps it was her birthday and this was her present? The catsuit too, perhaps. Kinky.

* * * * *

The library at night, with the fire crackling, with Wolfe in the big, old armchair, and myself sitting on the sofa with his sketches on my lap and a glass of wine in hand...it was eerie. Too quiet, too normal.

A snore interrupted my thoughts and I smiled. Lily was terribly amusing with her scatterbrained, doggy centering on her master – Wolfe. She'd adopted him and was curled up near his feet, in her makeshift bed made of old shirts and a towel.

Nine days left to go before I ran out of drug and nobody had turned up to claim her. So far I had kept Wolfe normal...relatively normal. I peeked at him. He was reading. A whole pile of books was at his elbow on the same table my wine glass used. To the side of the fireplace, the glass pane rattled and pattered with rain. A heavy storm had rolled in while we'd eaten supper. Roast beef and vegetables, all done in the wood-fired oven.

The tree limbs danced in the storm and the moonlight sent their straggly shadows swaying over our walls.

This situation was surreal.

Once upon a time...

Some mornings, I half expected to wake and find a thorn barrier growing out there, or for a little red riding hood to wander in and join us for breakfast.

I had the Wolfe already.

Difficult, to picture him at the rehab village. He had changed so much. His hair had seemed to take on a life of its own – stragglier, thicker, more beastlike. I could've sworn his shoulders were an inch wider too. No fangs yet, thank god. His cock might be bigger too. I snorted at that image popping into my head. Sex would be problematic, if he'd managed that.

Not that sex was likely.

I'd taken to masturbating whenever he wandered away, but it was a totally unfulfilled, unfinished sort of event. I couldn't come without him, it seemed. More than a few days, I'd flopped on my back on the bed, underwearless and frustrated, to swear at the ceiling. Maybe if I'd had a real vibrator I'd have vanquished my needs...maybe. I doubted it.

Sighing, I took a sip of wine, settled deeper into the musty upholstery then turned over the last sketch. Most were of me, naked or barely clothed. Somewhere inside, he harbored lustful thoughts. I smirked. I'd been startled when I'd seen the first few drawings but now I was used to being his subject, even if he had some whimsical imaginings, and some evil ones. This latest sketch, in particular. I wasn't sure I appreciated being turned into the elven slave of an orc...or whatever he was. The pointy ears looked fun, though, and I was slim yet had the largest boobs ever.

Three featured Lily. Lily asleep, upside-down and open mouthed, and no doubt snoring. Lily chasing a butterfly. Lily with a heap of weeds dangling from her mouth. She had an infuriating habit of bringing the outside things she found inside, then chewing them up.

"Come here."

That calm command had me raising my head to stare even as I put aside the sketches. He'd not bothered to command much at all, these past days.

I sauntered over, noticing how his gaze rested on my hips. The man was in there, still.

"Didn't you use to read this one? *The Princess Bride?*" He held up and waggled a hardback copy.

"Yes. A favorite of mine."

"The true romance did it for you?"

I smiled. "Everything. The movie made me hear all the dialogue in the book in the actors' voices."

"Yes, me too." He reached forward, took my hand, and pulled me until I sat on his lap. Then he recited, in a serious tone, "My name is Inigo Montoya. You killed my father. Prepare to die. That part I like."

"Mmm. Inconceivable." I did too but I liked sitting with him even more. He encompassed me, made me feel welcome. Loved? Like true love in *TPB*, as I called the book for short? Hell, no.

Wolfe thumbed open the pages as if to read from the book, with me sitting on him like a child being read to.

"True love," he murmured. "I remember you saying that, back then, at the rehab place."

Damn mind reader. Annoyed beyond reason, I wriggled and tried to stand.

"Stay." His arm went across my waist. "You know you can't go, unless I say."

Infuriating too. I puffed out my lips and stayed, slumping.

"What? You don't want to share the book?"

I shrugged. Our relationship had gone sideways. If he was my lover, maybe... How much had I changed to be thinking that? But he wasn't and that was my doing.

Lowering the dosage might trigger something like what'd happened the first day here. It might also give me a lover. Such a temptation. I ran my hand through my hair, untangling some knots as I sorted through my answer.

"Why don't you...make love to me anymore?" There, it was out.

"I'm not inclined."

"Inclined? How civilized of you." This was all my fault. If I had to be with him, why not have the fringe benefits?

Because, dumbass, he's dangerous.

"Does true love require fucking?" He pulled me so I rested on his chest and tilted back my head until we were eye to eye. The forest of his loose locks twined down, swaying, and his blue eyes hypnotized me. "You want kisses and caresses?"

"Yes." Exquisitely aware of his scent, his masculine presence, I sank deeper into desire with each rise and fall of my breasts. I swallowed. "Both?"

This was as far from true love as the sun from the moon. Which, scientifically was a long way. Romantically? I wasn't sure. They were kind of entangled in myth.

"Demanding woman."

Then he lowered his mouth to mine and kissed me – soft and sure, but without that wild force I craved. I twisted around to follow his mouth, and was left with my hand wrapped in his shirt when he drew away.

How did I come to crave what was bad for me?

I heard noises and looked up to see Lily scratching at the floor of the hallway. If she peed inside... I leapt up then looked back at Wolfe.

"Go."

I'd taken three strides toward her before the answer to one of the photos arrived. Amelia had stood exactly *there*. There'd been no rug on the floor as there was today. Lily had moved it with her scratching. Bare timber and the outline of what I now saw had been behind Amelia.

"Too late," I whispered.

A trapdoor. Lily had peed on a trapdoor.

From the creak of the floorboards, Wolfe approached. He threw the towel from Lily's bed over the puddle but shifted the cloth aside with his foot when he arrived.

"A trapdoor?"

"Uh huh. Did Magnus have a basement?"

"Probably. He was into creating a survival place, a fallout shelter."

"So, what's down there?"

"I don't know." He hauled on the recessed handle and pulled the trapdoor open. "I'll go look. You stay here."

It was dark, naturally, and metal stairs spiraled down.

"Truly?"

"Yes."

"But nothing is screeching at us or calling us to our doom. It's safe."

Wolfe chuckled. "I like your sense of humor, Kiara, but you stay."

"Pfft."

"I'll get a flashlight and you are to go sit and wait in the library."

I snorted. "Boring."

But I went and sat and I waited, twiddling my thumbs. When he emerged and closed the trapdoor, he wore a contemplative expression.

"Well?" I rose.

"I don't want you looking down there. Not unless I take you." His gaze was penetrating. "Understand?"

"Of course." How could I not? "How very cryptic. I *hate* mysteries."

"You'll survive." He nodded, as if to the tune of his thoughts. "Magnus had interesting tastes."

"Oh?" I raised an eyebrow nonchalantly – hoping for details.

"This is the fallout shelter to rival all fallout shelters."

"Now I'm even more curious. I'll wear a hole in my brain thinking about this. Tell me!"

"I know." He grinned evilly.

"Bastard."

His eyes took on an element of wickedness and he took a step my way, with the evil grin still plastered on. "That's not allowed."

"What isn't?" Mildly alarmed, I backed away. Then he advanced on me and I panicked – almost tripping over my feet as I tried to turn and run.

He could've told me to stay. He didn't. Instead his arm flashed out and he grabbed my wrist then towed me, protesting, to the armchair. When he sat and hauled me facedown over his lap, I knew what he intended.

"Hey! No spanking!"

"Says who? You don't get to call me bastard. Not today."

"What does today have to do with –"

But he was yanking down my shorts.

"It!" I clutched for the back of the shorts as they travelled over the widest part of my butt. The things were loose at my waist and with wriggling they came down without undoing anything, unfortunately. I grabbed for them, only to have Wolfe capture my hand and keep removing my shorts.

"Fuck! Hey!"

But this had become almost a game and I couldn't help giggling.

Despite a flurry of defensive maneuvers, I ended up bare-assed with both my wrists caught at the small of my back in one of his hands.

The first smack on my butt shivered a frisson of lust through me, straight to my pussy. Glorious. After smacking me, quite hard and painfully, a few more times, Wolfe shifted and when he spoke his words came from low down. I turned my head to look back at him and found he was inches away, watching.

The warmth of his exhalations, the burn of his weighty hands landing on me...I unraveled, pleasantly.

"You liked that, didn't you?"

"Um." I caught my lip in my teeth then let it slip. Truth? "Yes?"

There was pain but every blow had also sent my arousal soaring, had made me wetter. My entire body throbbed with the beat of my heart and the burn on my ass.

"Good." He slipped his hand between my open thighs then his finger wormed inside, slowly. Slow enough to melt my brain.

"Fuck," I whispered.

"I'm sure you want that, but not now. Let's just sit here for a while."

He what? Me lying with his finger in me? I was about to combust.

I wriggled and he shushed me, held me down and began to play.

"No talking."

I subsided. Within a minute I was ready to beg for more than what he was doing – working me into a mess, pushing his finger in and out while he held my cheeks apart, or bit me, or just held me down. He'd need a fire extinguisher soon.

Half an hour later – I wasn't sure of the time – I had bites all over my ass and three fingers inside me, and my poor clit was abused, what with all the grinding I'd tried to do against his thighs. I couldn't beg in words, but I'd done a ton of muted cursing and sobbing.

At last, he spoke. "I'm not going to fuck you. You're going to stand up and pull up your shorts and then we're going to read some of the book.

What did I have to do to get his cock in me? Pleading with my eyes didn't work either.

Desperate measures were needed.

The drug...I was going to do it. A little variation, a tiny drop. I would experiment.

Wolfe droned on, reading the book, toying with me still by simply being him – with his smell, his male bulk and hard muscles, and by squeezing me between his open legs. I'd ended up sitting there when he'd spread his legs. The chair was big enough. Surrounded by him again, only turned on to infinity and beyond.

Fuck this.

A small increment lower would be safe. Wolfe, a little crazier and with more libido. Yes. A little less drug might mean he'd want to tie me up. I tensed my thigh muscles, squirming, and my clit thanked me. After that, he could fuck me. That I could handle. Just so long as it wasn't as nasty as the other time.

Yet...I'd dreamed of being roped to that tree sometimes and woken with my hand between my legs. The man had screwed with my head.

Maybe hurting was what I really wanted? True lust, if not true love.

Lily was beside us, whining. I smiled. "Shhh, Lily."

She panted happily then lay down on the floor with her head on Wolfe's foot.

Talking to dogs – second sign of craziness. The first sign? I knew that one.

Desiring what might prove to be one's undoing? That was it.

God, I think I did want him to hurt me.

Again.

I almost began that night, when I poured him another glass of shiraz but decided to wait until the morning, when I hoped my hands wouldn't be shaking.

This could go so wrong, but I wanted to ride that burning line between death and glory.

* * * * *

Wolfe

Days ago, I'd recognized the taste of one of the drugs from the rehab center, in coffee of all things. It was bitter and distinctive. Maybe the concentration was higher and that triggered my memory, made me connect A to B? Either way, I knew.

So now, I waited. I wanted to see what she'd decide, though I'd pushed her tonight. I'd been impatient. The creep of things uncurling, walking about, feeling for her, in the back of my mind, it did get to me. I had kinky spiders under my stairs. Good ones if I could keep them in check. They fed a part of me that needed the taboo, the dark, the edginess. Only, I'd stay on *this* side of awareness. Forgetting most of the fucking of her was not good.

Now I knew what the drug did...I could add it to my armory. Use it.

When I wanted to, I could stop.

I wanted to see what she would do. Her cravings washed through her and registered way down in my balls. But I wasn't sure and I needed that surety.

I could recall fucking her though details were lost. Every second of the hour, of the day, I had the crawling sensation, the grabbing need, to take her. With the drug in my system, I could resist. I wanted *her* to decide to take the jump, didn't want to make her, or scare her into it.

If she didn't act soon, maybe I'd take back control. Or walk away. That possibility ate at me too. I needed *her.*

The drug made me lazy, but less crazy. And bad at rhyming.

I stalked her.

I waited.

Love had made me do this stupid thing. I think I'd loved her since forever...when she stepped into my room all those months ago.

What if she turned to the light and not the dark? Darth Vader wasn't every woman's love choice.

Letting her go would be difficult.

I was Wolfe. If the rest of my life didn't come back to me, I'd endure. Half the world was waiting to be my plaything. The best half, the female half.

Bullshit.

Just seeing her walk past made me ache. I'd be lost without her.

I'd come here to recover my past but this cabin yielded no answers. Even Magnus was a mystery. A friend, but why, when, how? Nothing I'd found in the cabin had said much.

Except perhaps the basement.

Things had stirred, my kinky spiders most of all, like they were reaching out and caressing all the gear he had down there – enough black leather and spiky stuff to start a heavy metal apocalypse. If this was Magnus's idea of a fallout shelter, I knew why I liked him.

Staying here forever, stalking Kiara, satisfied me. Moving on could wait. Making her mine was my aim and I could no longer do it without her consent.

I wanted to try out what was in the basement...on her.

True love didn't always look the same to everyone.

Inconceivable? No.

Love sometimes meant the cruelest torture.

CHAPTER 21

Doctor Hass

"So, this handwriting expert has decided this signature is an *M* and a *W*?"

The doctor inclined an eyebrow and managed to look at the sketch taken from the car and the officer at the same time, or so the officer thought. Maybe all medical professionals at this level were high functioning psycho-whatsits?

The police officer nodded. "Yes, sir."

"And why is this relevant? The man's been missing with the nurse for days now."

"He's committed alleged rape and sexual assault after being a patient with not an aggressive thought in his head for months. We need to know why. The alterations in his medications seem to not be enough of an explanation. Knowing everything we can may facilitate his capture, sir. You submitted a report that said you didn't believe he was Andy Carruthers. We've tracked down men from his unit as well as the relative, Andy's father, who turned out to be a homeless man. We showed them recent photos. They all swore that Wolfe is not Andy. We've put his DNA through the police database and got nothing. Who do you think he is?"

"*M.W.* That signature is fascinating. He claimed to be named Wolfe, in some early assessments made. He was ignored." The doctor looked up at the officer and tapped the sheet of paper on his desk. "It seems likely the *W* would be for Wolfe. I've also tried to get his

DNA checked by some less forthcoming secret intelligence and quasi military organizations of this glorious nation of ours. They did diddly squat for me. If you help, perhaps this can go higher. Perhaps..." The doctor leaned back into his padded chair. "We can find out who this man really is?"

"FBI? CIA? NSA?"

"And any other acronyms that you can think of. I'm sure we have ones I don't know about."

"That sounds like a good idea. I'll pass it on upward." The police officer held out his hand and Dr. Hass shook it. "Thank you for your co-operation, doctor."

"You're welcome. I have to admit this man makes me extremely curious. I like having my facts straight and his are damn well crooked as all hell."

* * * * *

Damian
A motel in Minnesota

"There!" He tapped the map where the download feed had updated. The drone overfly had finally picked them up. "A weak signal but it is there."

"Well now. That's remarkable. Good lithium battery!" Guera had a spoonful of breakfast oatmeal in hand. Carefully she set the bowl on the table and came to Damian where he sat on the bed. "Have you the exact coordinates yet?"

"Soon. Even if we don't find it again, we have an approximate location. This seems correct. The car registration was tracked to a town that's a two-hour drive away."

"Weeks ago."

"True, but it was the last location found. There's not much up there on the mountain. If the car's there, they might be. Such a remote position will be an advantage. Less interference. And see how good my hunch was..." He moved the mouse cursor and circled a road. "Here was where that strange double killing happened."

"Yes. You are a *very* clever man."

"I'm concerned that the doctor won't come here to take the sample, and of course Wolfe is likely going to be too aware by now for us to transport him far."

"Yes. Yes. It will be a problem. I don't want to be arrested going across state lines with a handcuffed man in the back of our vehicle."

"No. And if half of the myths about him are true, he's not someone we should take lightly. The woman is likely dead by now. But, we'll figure this out when we need to. We have the tissue sample kit."

"Ugh. I'd rather just kill a man and bury him than this." She screwed up her nose. "Brains? Makes me feel like I am a zombie."

"But a pretty one! And now, we wait." Damian put the laptop aside and lay on his back on the bed. He shuffled his cellphone from his pocket. "I have a jigglypuff hatching soon. We should go for a walk."

Gueara tsked but lay down beside him. "Just so you can catch a new Pokémon?"

"Of course." Tongue out, he winked at her. "Perhaps I could catch you instead while we wait for a triangulation on the flyover?"

She turned onto her stomach and propped herself on her elbows. "You have the best ideas. I can be your jiggle puff?"

"Jiggly. Hmm." He reached and caressed beneath her breast, weighing it gently and smoothing his fingers over the fabric of her top. "Depends. I think I need to see you hatch an egg first."

"Haha. I think I should wrestle you for that. I win, *you* hatch an egg, from your butt, sir."

Damian leaped off the bed then poised himself like a sumo wrestler about to strike. "On the count of three. One, two..."

"Three!"

Laughing they toppled onto each other and rolled on the bed, slowly stripping each other of clothing.

When his phone beeped out a Pokémon notification, they were both too busy kissing to bother checking.

CHAPTER 22

Wolfe

Kiara had lowered the dose of the drug. Once suppertime had come and gone, I was certain. Her allure had never dissipated, but instead of being willing to appreciate and not fuck, now I was thoroughly interested in mounting her on my cock and screwing her into the floor.

Gently, gently, my new mindset told me.

Whatever else this drug had done, it'd given me back my smarts.

The writhing spider things, the tentacles, whatever lived at the back of my head – those never went away. Unlike before, I aimed not to tear both of us apart.

That was the trick. The right amount of drug balanced me on the edge.

"Come."

"What?" Kiara kept pouring scotch and didn't look at me, quite. Nervous? Inside her head, she was twangier than a wound-up guitar string.

"All I need is you." I took the glasses of wine and the scotch from her and placed them on the counter top then led her by the hand into the library.

Her blue dress was some heavy yet soft material that flared and swished around her legs at mid-thigh. I rested an appreciative hand on her lower back to guide her.

She had an inkling of what this meant. After all, she'd given me the lower dose.

I'd suggested the dress for tonight and some pretty lace underwear. A woman in the town had gone shopping elsewhere and brought clothes back for me.

The fire was stoked high, the room warm enough to get naked.

I sat on the sofa and drew her to me, to stand while I ran my hands up the backs of her thighs until I found her ass.

"Eighth wonder of the world. I could feel your ass all day."

Nervous, she smiled back.

Nothing, not even my cock, was telling me what to do tonight. Slowly, letting both of us soak into the pleasure of the moment, I smoothed my hands over her – her ass then her back, before running my fingers between her legs over the lace, then back to squeezing her ass again. Toying with her.

When she'd relaxed, with a small curve forming on her parted lips and her hands resting on my shoulders, when her body followed my hands, begging for more, I spoke quietly.

"I know you've been feeding me a drug to stop me going too crazy." She tried to step away but I shook my head and she subsided. Her teeth snagged a corner of her lip.

"I can feel your fear. You think I'll punish you? No."

"Why?" came out squeaky and she tried again. "Why?"

"Because I want to love you and not destroy you. That's your doing." I leaned back and just held her hands by the fingertips. "I'm thinking straight again. I know who I am." When her mouth fell open, I shook my head. "Not that. No. I mean I understand myself and what might happen. I want to make love to you, nicely, not half kill you. I want us both to like it."

Her mouth made an *O* of astonishment. I put my finger across her lips.

"Yes. But what you like isn't simple, is it?"

"I..." She looked down at where I held her fingers. Her mouth writhed. "I don't know."

"I do. I have *some* memories. I remember you loving some of the dirtiest things. And I know what's in here." My lips twisted in amusement as I stroked the side of her forehead. "That's okay because I like my love-making dirty too."

Her frown was cute enough to make me want to kiss it away.

"If I make you hurt while I fuck you, you'll like that."

With my hands on her back, I drew her between my legs.

Her hand went to where I was kneading her ass, to cover my hand, to feel me, and her throat moved in a swallow of arousal. "Maybe."

"Maybe? Lying isn't allowed." I pulled my hand from beneath hers to grab the back of her thigh. My fingers pushed between her legs, forcing the material of her dress in there too. Through the dress, my thumb stroked her skin. "I've not been in control of myself before, or not for long. I want to play you like an instrument." I pinched her thigh and held it, while her grimace become a small sigh. Such a cute liar. "Like a maestro with a beautiful violin he wants to hear make beautiful sounds. Well-fucked sounds, in your case. And then..."

She'd been listening, avidly, but I stopped. Wait. Wait... Telling her I loved her should wait.

"And then?"

"Such bright eyes. Such nice wriggling." I reinforced my possession of her thigh by shifting my grip and squeezing her hard. "Shhh now, until I say to talk."

Her hair was twisted into a bun. I held her neck to pull her down to my mouth then kissed her softly. The sigh of air from her lips was harsher than my kissing. Impatient, she tried to pounce on my mouth.

"No. You will wait."

The bun unraveled under my fingers and her hair spilled loose in waves of black. I kissed her again as I drew the shoulders of her dress down her arms. Then I bared her breasts, slipping them from the cups of her bra.

"Pretty tits."

She grunted, unhappy.

"Don't like that?"

At the wrinkling of her forehead, I chuckled. Underneath her annoyance she was pleased. Mild objectification was something she liked.

Which only made me wonder if heavy objectification worked as well. Had I tried that already and forgotten?

"What would turn you on? Being fucked with your head in stocks? Or collared and leashed and tied to the floor? Hmmm?"

At my suggestions, her mind had turned into chaos. Aroused, scared, but mostly aroused.

Below each breast, I ran a finger along the bunched material of the bra cups. I lowered my head then used my finger grip to tug each breast toward my mouth. I teased and licked, nipped. Kissing her nipples until they shrank and hardened into nubs gave me a bite-able target then a whimpering girl.

My teeth on her nipple, stretching it outward then releasing it, before I sucked, made her squirm so much. I had to wrap my hand around her breast to keep her from moving away.

Already, she was so worked up she was glazed of eye.

Only then did I encourage her dress to slip down her body. The cloth caressed her curves, as it flowed then puddled around her ankles.

My mouth found the lacy triangle of her panties. I kissed her mound through them and bit her. Her moans and breathy sighs became louder, her hands tangled in my hair and urged my head toward her again.

Tsking, I straightened then I removed her bra. "If you can't be still, I need to tie your hands. Turn."

"Um." She dithered, maybe dumbstruck by my lack of force, of command. I only waited. Eventually she gave in and shuffled around to present her wrists at her back.

Two, crossed wrists.

A simple thing that said so much.

The headiness of her obeying me was almost as good...I halted in thought. As good as forcing her to. Better? I wasn't sure. The flurry of cruel desires at the edges of my mind made that a hard one to compare. The things within me lusted. Were they me or something foreign, alien? One day, I'd discover this. Not now. I shoved them away then twined the blue bra around her wrists and knotted it, firmly.

Take care, I reminded my tamer brain. Her hands needed blood.

Just seeing her fingers wrapped in each other and the tie on her wrists made my dick harder.

Not once had I commanded her. This night must be ours, our desires entangled.

Tied up, quiet – apart from a few moans, and ready for me to do what I wanted. What was in the basement wanted exploring...

That could come later. Much, much later.

Rolling her panties down until her slit was reachable, seeable, lickable, that came next. "Are you wet enough?"

She tossed her hair as if to say no, and I snorted. "Liar. Just for that I'm using the steel-spiked dildo on you when we go downstairs."

Her gasp of indignation made me grin.

That sounded fun, if only I knew where that was. Was it real? I hadn't seen one when cleaning.

The dark things writhed, beckoned. I was certain a dildo with faux steel spikes was down there, in a drawer.

Was my memory was coming back? Magnus and I must've played with women together. Of all the things to forget.

A steel-pronged wooden dildo... The spikes dithered between real and not-real in my memory. I knew which I'd prefer.

This was supposed to be nice fucking.

Test her boundaries. One never knew if one didn't try, especially where dildos with spikes were concerned.

"Wolfe –" she began.

"Didn't I say no more talking?" I reached out mentally.

She shushed. Sometimes it was best to enforce orders.

CHAPTER 23

Kiara

If Wolfe bit and pulled on the skin of my butt one more time, my eyes would pop. My nipples still burned with what he'd done to them. *Fuck*. My heart was throbbing fast as could be. My breathing was hoarse in my ears. Though he'd stopped me talking, he'd left me freedom to do or not do, to think, or not think, in every other way. And I was still turned on beyond belief.

Freedom, a novel concept where he was concerned.

I tested the binding on my wrists and was tempted to get loose. It would mean the destruction of the bra but...oh my, the idea undid me. I pulled and twisted, wrenched, and something snapped behind my back. Grinning devilishly, I reached blindly and grabbed his hair.

"Ah-huh." His matter-of-fact tone was unnerving, and more than a little diabolical, but I hung on.

Until...he took hold of my wrists again, bit my ass even harder. I squeaked out a bitten-off stream of *noes* that weren't quite the finished word and sounded like panicked grunts – which they were. Not talking was bizarrely elevating my arousal. Finally, after one last shudder, I ceased squirming and waited for him to release my flesh.

With his fingers gentle on my hips, he turned me to face him.

"Naughty. Now you see what happens when you deliberately rip through bondage I place on you."

With little effort, he picked me up, bodily, to arrange me stomach down over the arm rest of the sofa with my arms in front and my hands clasped. He entwined my fingers with each other, one by one, as if they were some intricate puzzle.

Kneeling, he delivered his next words from inches away. His finger pressed on my nose. "Don't move, at all, while I decide on your punishment."

God. The word *punishment* had jellied into me, heated and laden with a delicious sort of scariness. What was he planning?

Everything he did to me tonight had a sexual context, an overtone. That enthralled me. Or rather, he did. *Wolfe.*

How apt that he had the name of a predatory animal.

Even thinking of his name, *Wolfe,* in the privacy of my head inclined me to shivering. Now that he was controlling himself, his presence had a potency that stamped itself on the very air I breathed. I inhaled his power, got off on it, because I was his focus.

"Understand?"

I nodded and I licked my lips, ending up with my tongue tip seemingly glued to my upper lip because foggy thoughts of punishment were whizzing about in my head, until he smirked at me. I sucked my tongue back in and tried to look blasé, despite being ass up over a sofa.

"Good." He rose to his feet and walked away.

Then he began to amass a collection of things on the sofa before me. After some puzzlement, I realized all of them could plausibly be used on my rear end.

A book, a hardback, was placed there. A curtain cord. His belt. What looked like a stick. A spatula from the kitchen. Last of all, he walked over with something long and thin that had him examining it before he reverently positioned it on the upholstery.

In the firelight, with reflections making one side of it gleam, was the iron fire poker. *Jesus H...*that was metal.

His expression was contemplative, as if using it was a possible.

No way. I cleared my throat and his gaze flashed to me – a beast spotting a meal that squeaked.

Shocked, I froze.

He was being nice, he'd said. Was that even possible with this man?

CHAPTER 24

Wolfe

The look on her face, after I placed the poker on the sofa, priceless.

"You think I won't use it?"

She made some small sound so I crouched and shifted the poker closer to her. The poker was heavy, rusty, lethal looking – all the elements that made my balls happy.

Resist.

Oh, I would. I just loved her expression.

"I can imagine the effect on you, even if used lightly. The bruises... Perhaps it would be the right punishment? Or would you rather this?" I retrieved the stick instead. The poker would be an assault rather than a sadistic pain that might enhance her pleasure, but the mind fuck was awesome...because, she almost believed me.

Yes. The whisper of the word echoed in my head.

There was something wrong with that and I couldn't quite put my finger on it. Her, though, I could definitely finger her.

I stood with the stick in hand, swished it back and forth. "Maybe later? We can toy with the poker later."

Fingering. *Hmmm.* I wriggled the cloth of her panties down again. Somehow she'd righted them after I'd exposed her before. "Did you pull these up when I wanted to see your pussy? Damn. Double punishment. Next time, don't."

Her gasp at the first strike seemed the beginning of my concerto.

I remembered my aim – this night was for both of us. And that I loved her. So I switched her ass red, leaving a few stripes and scratches, then I bit her to make her wriggle, then I fucked her with my fingers.

If only I had that dildo.

Her pussy was dripping already. I pulled her panties all the way down, lifted each foot off the rug to strip them from her. The crotch was wet and they'd not even been in contact with her pussy while I'd been switching her.

Such a pretty, moaning, and quivering wreck. Such a striped ass. I drew a fingernail down a few of the stripes to see her twitch and moan. And I'd barely begun.

"Still making noises?" I whispered. "Open your mouth."

I leaned over her.

Tears had dribbled from the corners of her eyes.

While I stuffed the panties past her lips, I licked at the tears and kissed her cheek. The belt would be sexy wrapped across her mouth and buckled, but I wanted to use it. So I wound the curtain cord around her face and across her mouth to stop her spitting out the panties. I was careful. Swallowing the cloth would be bad so I wedged part of them between the cord and her lips. She shook her head as if to dislodge the impromptu gag and I shushed her.

"It stays. Be good and I'll be nicer."

I'd even used a slip-knot at the back of her head so I could remove the gag, fast, if necessary.

Yes, I was nice and safety conscious. If only the poker didn't catch my eye. It was the equivalent of a rearing cobra – deadly, but fascinating in its terrible beauty.

I wiped my forehead with the back of my arm. It was a sweaty business, making a woman scream. My cock was throbbing painfully, so I stripped, and once I had my dick in hand, what else could I do except the obvious?

Her mouth was taken. I hadn't thought that one through now, had I?

I crouched beside the sofa again. "Want to get fucked now, Kiara?" With my finger, I traced the outside of the cord where it dug into her face, her lips where they still showed, around her eyes, then along from one eyebrow to the other.

She hadn't made a noise and seemed hypnotized. The pain had affected her, and the dominance. I reached beneath and squeezed her nipple between finger and thumb until she jerked and whimpered. "Want to get fucked?"

Her nod was accompanied by such a cute admission of hunger in her brown eyes that I relented, releasing her nipple to kiss her gagged mouth. "Good girl."

I went around behind her, let my cock find her pussy, and nudged inside a half-inch. The feel of that made me close my eyes for a second. But...

Her ass was raised and begging, her hands were free and clutching at the sofa in anticipation. My forehead wrinkled. That wouldn't do.

So I left her there and descended to the basement where I found the pair of leather cuffs I recalled. These, she wouldn't tear loose from. They had tiny padlocks. The key – I might need that. No pockets on me, since I was naked, so I left the key on the hook on the wall. Then I ascended the spiral stairs and returned to her.

"Not moved? You're learning. Put your hands at your back." I locked her wrists into the cuffs and connected them, locked that too.

This time I drew my cock up and down her slit, until lubricated with her wetness, then I guided myself in, slow as the clench and release of her pussy on me, and even slower when she gripped me tighter. There was agony in making her wait, for both of us, but I stalled and toyed with the switch marks on her butt.

When I had her making small passionate noises and curving toward my pain and not away, I shoved in all the way. I fucked her until she was on tiptoes, struggling to angle her ass into my thrusts, then I pulled out and kneeled behind her. With three fingers, I impaled her, widening her entrance, stretching it this way and that while I talked quietly.

Her gag-muffled whimpers and the haze of lust rising in her mind told me I was definitely doing what turned her on, as did the wetness welling past my fingers.

"I'm not going to fuck you properly for ages. I forbid you to come, Kiara, but you can come as close..." I wormed those fingers in, full depth, then pulled out and sneaked in the fourth. Then I left them there so she was painfully full. "You can get as close to climax as you can. But *don't* come."

I made that a command. Then I waited with my four fingers penetrating her until she emerged from her dazed state.

Finally, she nodded, grunted, a reply.

"Good."

The removal of my fingers left her slumped into the sofa and panting. Her ass swayed in an invitation. With my palms on her inner thighs, I pushed her legs wide and commenced my torture of her clit. I licked her, sucked on it, played with that nub with the tip of my tongue, then sucked on it again with greater suction.

Her squeaking made me stop and grin.

"Almost coming?"

"Mmm!"

I chuckled. I knew anyway, could tell easily.

So I abused her clit some more.

Earlier, she'd showered in our rainwater and she tasted fresh, and only of her own juices. I gathered some on my palm and massaged back and forth over the lips of her pussy then higher, circling, squashing down. I stuck my tongue inside her while I pinched her swollen clit.

She was reduced to muttering groans and mangled words that sounded like the beginning of *stop* as she wriggled and rocked.

Laughing at her probably wasn't registering, but I enjoyed seeing her desperate, especially when I stopped moving to watch her futilely impale her cunt on my fingers.

A few times, I stuck my cock in her and fucked her, until my own desire to come was near bursting. The last time, I withdrew, and turned her over so she presented her sex to my view...and her breasts. Everywhere I'd sucked or bitten or smacked was a blushing red.

"Don't move," I said, my voice low and threatening. "Not an inch."

The switch, where I'd left it on the sofa, tempted me again. I swiped some lighter, burning lines across the underside of each breast. Her yelps from behind the gag were enticing as fuck.

"Christ, you tempt me. I'd come if I fucked you now."

She pouted and squirmed, spreading her legs...and with her hands bound and under her. The sight of a bound woman pleading for sex never got old. Her mouth, if I took off that gag, was available for fucking too.

I narrowed my eyes. "Little bitch. God *damn*. You can wait."

When she came. I would too. It was *The Plan*, highlighted, underlined, engraved on my brain.

Too easy to do her now, to lose myself. So I switched her thighs for tempting me. Then I ate her out again, made sure she reached to the *very* top in arousal, and I kept her there, panting and incoherent with the desire to go over.

I let her quieten, and did it again. In between I flipped her over and paddled her with the book, a hardback copy of *The Princess Bride*. It seemed apt, funny, and made her butt redder.

My hands shook. I stared at them until they settled, then sniffed in a long breath and wiped away more sweat. With my fist around my cock, I circled the sofa.

When she could see me, her gaze latched on. I was her messiah, her Bringer of Pleasure, her Beast. I'd wear all those labels proudly.

"What do you want, Kiara? Say it."

She coughed around the gag. *You* came out as *ooo*, but I translated well.

"You want to be fucked? Where? Your ass?"

The *no* was quite clear and I grinned. "Okay, no more talking. But, I just put a big tick next to defiling you everywhere. Now I *know* I'm fucking your ass tonight."

Her indignant hiccup, as she tried to speak, then her scowl, made my grin widen.

I'd calmed, so I put a knee on the sofa near her head and undid the gag, removed the panties, then stuffed my cock into her willing mouth for several strokes. There were liquid, squishy noises as my cock travelled deep, almost fucking down her throat. When my balls squeezed in, I pulled free and staggered back, leaving her to splutter.

My own breathing was hurried.

Preoccupied, I drifted my gaze to that poker.

No.

I swallowed, needing to distract myself from using it.

"Time to go downstairs, Kiara. Let's see your other presents. Maybe you'll get to come."

Though deeply aroused, she managed an eye roll or two and stuck her tongue out at me, waggled it.

Her sense of humor was intact. So was mine.

I put my forehead to hers. "There are clamps down in the basement that fit tongues." When her tongue was abruptly sucked back in, I winked. "Not joking."

I pulled the cord from her neck then dragged her to her feet. The only other object I took with us to the stairs was that poker. When I dropped it down the stairwell, the clang and clatter as it bounced off the metal rungs would have awoken the dead.

Down there, held such promise.

My toes hung over the edge. I had her by the neck. She wasn't leaving and I took a moment to think and look down through the square hole.

I'd left the lights on and they blazed in my eyes, blinding me in specks where the light flared off metal.

Shiny things were there.

And the poker now lay quiet, a straight line on the floor.

If nothing else, it reminded her, and me, of possibilities.

The hand with which I'd held the poker shook but stilled when I willed it so.

I hadn't yet told her to speak fully and from how she'd trembled and leaned into my body as we'd walked, letting her stay silent was best. It made her terribly submissive – just how I liked her.

"Shut your eyes and don't open them until I say. I'll guide you."

Her hands were locked at her back, but I could take her weight if she slipped.

She'd be fine, at least until her feet reached the floor below.

CHAPTER 25

Kiara

"Shut your eyes." I hated that. Going down an unknown spiral staircase with Wolfe holding my bound wrists from below, since he'd gone first – it was fraught with danger. Despite the molten desire he had summoned with pain and pleasure... And *how* I remembered that.

While I sprawled on the sofa, mouth, stick, fingers, and cock, were used on me, in me, repeatedly. But I could think now. There'd been time for the stings and bruises to quieten, for all the swollen parts of me to lessen and stop crying for attention. Though I craved and hurt, I could think.

The Keppra.

The shock of realization was so great I almost opened my eyes.

But I kept going down, turning in that spiral, step after step.

The third dose of the day had been in the scotch. I hadn't realized he intended some marathon sex session or I'd have blurted out a warning while I was still allowed to speak.

If this kept on for too long, he'd sink into his beast state.

I had to warn him.

How?

Then we reached the bottom, my feet felt the softness of rug on rock or irregular concrete. What a mammoth and insane effort it must've taken to create this room.

As my thoughts churned and I struggled with speaking when I was not to do so, leather curled and was fitted snugly about my neck.

A buckle jingled as it was fastened. Leather was wrapped and locked about my ankles.

I shivered at the possession this signified.

"Got you," Wolfe murmured, his voice rolling in, drawn from the abyss.

That assurance was such a turn on that more of my wetness seemed to dribble from me and onto my thigh. My knees gave way for a second. As I straightened, I inhaled, smelling him and his sweat, as well as the sweetness of near ecstasy.

He'd let me come now wouldn't he? He'd fuck me?

With his hand gripping my neck and all the other accessories he'd applied to me, thoughts were jumbling, tumbling. *Keppra. Remember?*

Yes.

No more of this teasing with hands or cock or tongue, please. But I squeezed my thighs together at that memory. He'd left me writhing, wanting, throbbing.

My pussy felt ten times more swollen and sensitive than ever before. If he so much as touched me there...

He slapped his hand over my pussy and I doubled over. So close.

Then...

From behind, he lifted me and forced his cock in. Past my nothing defense in seconds. Crammed in. Fucking me in piston moves. I screamed, mouth wide. *God.* The pulse and the stretch of my walls.

A storm rose in an instant.

Penetrated, I could only gasp, almost soundless, but my temples beat like a drum with the rhythm of my blood. Waiting, waiting for more. Magic.

Though he held me in place, I writhed, feeling that circle of flesh clamped onto him.

"God, you feel good." Then he sucked himself out of me.

Gone. Empty. It was a happening as serious as the withdrawal of a sword from flesh. I sobbed and collapsed to my knees, only caught at the last moment by his hands. As my knees met rug, I barely made a bump. A second later my forehead touched.

Then he was in me again, filling me.

My throat closed. The change from nothing to everything. From denied, to *his.*

And he didn't stop. The fucking went on – driving me forward, my forehead sliding, breasts swaying, and him slapping into my ass as he slammed in.

My body, my mind, reached higher, lust brimming at the very edge of eruption.

"Come." His grunted command freed me. I tumbled into climax, mind annihilated as I strained and spasmed. Legs wide, fucked, with him coming inside me and his hard-muscled arms locked through mine and holding me...*tight.*

I slumped, allowed at last to spill onto the rug, sliding into a heap in spite of his cum leaking from inside me.

I was ready to sleep, to drowse, to spoon. His pain and dominance had never inhibited my arousal, it was what I needed. I saw that now.

Without it, love-making would be as ephemeral as a breeze, near worthless.

My mind made itself anew from the jigsaw pieces. *Keppra,* I remembered.

I tried speaking, and still couldn't.

Blindly, I sought him. He wasn't touching me. I heard water running before he walked over and helped me to my feet.

"Fuck, you slay me," he grated out. "Needed to get one fuck in..."

He wrapped a hand over one breast and squeezed.

I grunted at the pain, the feel of him handling what was his.

"...before I do more."

More?

No. He *had* to let me speak.

But he only kissed me, hard, then pulled me to a new part of the room, tied my hands to the ceiling, and my legs to the floor and spread wide.

I couldn't stop him and I so needed to.

We both might die. I wished I'd told him of my deception. Wished I'd blurted the truth when he took the drinks from my hand.

I'd forgotten that once he gained momentum the need to fuck consumed him. Trembling, I flexed my hands and tested the leather surrounding my wrists. Blind, mute, and fastened in place, I feared the coming of his beast. I waited for what seemed an eternity, ticking off time with the thuds of my pulse.

"Open your eyes."

Thank god. Maybe he'd let me speak too.

I opened my eyes. Mouth set, eyes fiercely attentive, he approached me with some wooden thing. A spear? My heart skittered. *No.* It wasn't. Relief was short-lived. He carried a huge dildo with spikes, mounted on what might be a broom handle. Lube glistened on the end that was clearly meant to go inside me. As he came nearer I saw that the spikes weren't metal and were probably painted nubs.

Still, that thing was big.

I quailed and tried to shrink away, but the cuffs held me in place.

This wasn't *nice.* I shook my head, fast enough to dizzy myself. Wolfe ignored my sounds of protest and went around behind me.

As the tip of the dildo touched my entrance and began to slide in, so stiff and unyielding that my flesh could barely move aside enough to allow it access, he spoke.

Head back, mouth taut, my hands in fists to resist the pain, I listened.

"Want to see this in you. Want to fuck you too."

He bit the angle of my neck, once, and I screeched.

I'd jammed my eyes shut, futile maybe, but instinctive.

Anything to get away from the inexorable advance, the expanding pain.

His guttural, primitive words awoke my brain. He was descending into the beast. Frantic to break something, I clutched the chain above the cuffs and pulled myself upwards until my legs were taut.

His hand slammed onto my shoulder and hauled me down and that thing he wielded rotated and tunneled into me.

No escape. Panting, I subsided, whining, letting him do this, enduring.

When he stopped, the dildo felt halfway to my heart. My pussy attempted to clench and failed. I grimaced. Gasping through jammed-together teeth, I looked down while blinking away tears and sweat.

Between my legs the butt end of the stick showed, wedged to the floor. He adjusted the length, twisting the handle.

Fuck. Speared. Trapped. With that thing in me, and the cuffs, I wasn't going anywhere fast.

Yet he had worse. Wolfe wrapped his hands over my hips and prodded my ass with his erection – yet more proof he was changing. He could fuck for hours while like this.

Slowly, he screwed himself inside me, grunting and shunting back and forth by micro fractions as my ass relaxed enough, barely, to let him in.

Not fast enough it seemed. For the first time this night, he spilled his power into me.

Ohmigod. I sucked air and groaned as a climax stormed in, shuddering through my muscles, throwing me outside reality for crucial seconds, minutes.

When I returned to awareness, Wolfe was deep within and I rocked back and forth to the slow fucking of my ass.

Nothing could beat this.

I loved it. I hated it. I wanted him deeper, harder, even if it tore me up.

When he came, he was buried in me to the hilt and the swell of his cum compelled me to shove my ass backward as much as I could, fastened, cuffed, and impaled as I was.

Sweat slicked us both.

Our breathing and the drum of my heart filled the room.

The undoing of chains and ties, the removal of the dildo, let me fall boneless to the floor. I curled up and listened to him pacing and growling.

Words...

To get him to take the Keppra, I needed words. I had none.

Tears overflowed then trickled from my eyes.

He hauled me to my feet and over his shoulder then, like some clone of King Kong, he walked to the spiral staircase and began to climb.

CHAPTER 26

Wolfe

When I reached the room above, I pushed her into the wall, then pushed my cock into her again.

Her skin scintillated under my touch. Colors rose. She felt like velvet and butterflies, like summer raindrops on my tongue. Though standing, I fell, my mind tumbling endlessly.

It tripped me into a memory.

This was a part of me that I didn't want.

I shoved away, my dick pulling from her ass, and staggered backward.

Love, *nice*, remember?

But she tempted me so.

I'd locked the cuffs at her back. The memory of being inside her, of coming... *God. Damn.*

I turned away and found myself faced with my hunting knife, stark upon the kitchen counter.

Man...

The knife... I grabbed it, spread my palm upon the counter, flat, aimed between the long bones, and nailed it there with the knife.

The pain flared through me.

For a few seconds, I collapsed to my knees, despite the drag of the blade in my hand.

Gasping, tears pouring, I pulled myself upright.

Tablets, right?

I didn't know why I'd done this, thought she had the dose figured.

She was wrong maybe.

Her handbag was miles away. I wasn't courageous enough to unnail my hand. I'd never regain control if I went to her again. I stretched, the pain making me pant, found her bag, and dragged it across the counter until I had it before me.

Fuck.

Forehead to the counter, I took a second.

There was blood. I knew this.

Ignore.

I gritted my teeth and pawed at her bag, found the zipped up pocket. *Tablets.* Punching out those took me longer than a NASA scientist plotting a moon landing but the pain helped me focus.

Done.

I stared at the tablets and stuffed two or three of them into my mouth, chewed the fucking things and swallowed them.

Then...I slumped, falling to the floor with my hand above, nailed there.

Kiara was on the other side of the room, cuffed still, hands at her back and looking weary and thoroughly defiled.

What had I done?

"Sorry," I croaked.

She was Bambi in the headlights. Her legs were trembling.

"Sit," I told her.

She shook her head violently.

"Suit yourself." My hand was throbbing like someone had filled it full of bees and set it on fire. When she only grunted, I blinked and worked through the logic. "Talk. When you want to."

"You're bleeding."

I shrugged, then regretted it as more pain tore in. "I'd never have guessed. I heal. It's nothing."

There was dubiousness in her tilted eyebrows and frown lines.

"Why?"

Should I say? She'd probably guessed. "To stop myself getting to you, and it cleared my head, woke me."

Wouldn't have worked forever though, the pain. A stab wound, I just knew I'd have shrugged it off after the sharper pain ebbed. This way, if I moved at all, there'd be new cutting, new pain.

Though I tried not to dwell on her being naked and bound only a few yards away, the vision drew me. Those plump breasts, and the pretty circles of her nipples were like targets for my mouth, my hands, my teeth. I could see teeth marks on her, red as well as faint, stippled purple.

Groaning, I ducked my head, ran my free hand over my face, peered out at her through the cage of my fingers.

Fuck. She had my cum on her legs.

The tablets would take time to work. Time. Needed time. I could pull out the knife.

No.

Blood was running down my arm.

If I stood the pain would lessen. If I stood, I might leap at her.

Before I succumbed to either the tablets or some dreadful beast rage, I said the words I should've said earlier, "I love you."

Her stare of incomprehension floored me.

What else did I expect?

CHAPTER 27

Kiara

I sighed, exasperated, horrified, annoyed even. After he'd stabbed himself, I wasn't sure I'd blinked for a whole minute. Like a gruesome monument, the knife stood up where he'd plunged it through his hand and into the counter. Lucky he was too stupid, as he was, to pluck out the blade.

The blood on his arm was in layers due to all the jerking about he'd done – drying, clotting, and fresh, wet blood.

He was still bleeding but wasn't moving, though his chest rose and fell.

I hadn't dared to approach, but now, maybe it was safe?

I'd watched him go through phases, from aware and somewhat smart, to barbaric and lusting after me to the point of almost ripping off his hand. Having him standing there, unable to get at me, with a rampant erection had been weirdly breathtaking. He'd pull at his hand, roar at the pain, then try again. Now, he was dull-eyed and unresponsive.

He'd ingested too much Keppra for his system, especially considering that idiosyncratic reaction he had to the drug. I knew what I needed to do.

My nursing instincts nudged me.

And my fears... What should be driving me from him was also driving me toward him – to pull out that knife and make sure he didn't die from an overdose, infection, or blood loss.

Didn't want him to die; didn't want him to leave my world.

"Complicated," I muttered. "Damn you."

Could I do anything? My arms were getting uncomfortable, pulled back the way they'd been for ages. I poked the wall behind me with my fingers, walking them along.

He'd hurt himself to stop himself from hurting me...okay, hurting me more.

To be honest, though shaken and scared, I wasn't sure when I'd have stopped him, given a choice. Not after what'd happened up here, for certain. Downstairs? Hmmm. I guess I was one fucked-up, kinky bitch. No one could *ever* approach the effect he had on me. Wolfe making love to me was a mixture of walking on a volcano's edge and being in a porno movie where the orgasms were real.

I sniffed.

I was covered in mess, sore, weak-headed even. If I went too close to him and he turned beast again, I couldn't bear to imagine what would happen.

I took a hesitant step forward and waited to see if he'd lunge for me.

Brave. Stupid. Caring. Intelligent, half the time. He was all those. And, I frowned, he thought he was in love with me. Those quiet words had taken a second to translate, being so foreign to my understanding. This wasn't exactly a romantic interlude in Paris with champagne, lobster, and rubbery sex toys.

I sucked in my lip, concerned about what he might do, but most of all, for his well-being. Surprising but inevitable. He'd permeated the very molecules of my soul. It wasn't just the lunatic level sex, it was who he was when he was, well...normal. And it wasn't as if that state wasn't achievable and repeatable.

Just needed the drug, was all.

Yes, we'd both messed up, but it was what he did when brought to the brink of destruction that had truly shaken my notions about where I stood in his world.

Stuck that knife in his hand. *Jesus.*

After one deep, steadying breath, I walked to him.

By the last step, I was sure he was unconscious. If he stopped breathing, there was nothing much I could do, except knee him. *What a pickle.* The knife was imbedded at the very edge of the counter. If it hadn't been, his arm could never have been positioned as it was.

Luckily, or maybe it was deliberate, the sharp edge faced away from the window, so his jumping about hadn't dragged the steel all the way through his hand.

There might be a way to remove it, if I was gymnastic. I just had to jump backward onto the counter without knifing myself, falling, or knocking myself out.

After three dramatic tries, and almost sliding off due to the blood under my ass, I managed. I examined the knife and how he'd stuck it between the metacarpal bones. Wriggling the steel loose from the timber top was going to be harder to do than getting my ass up here. Slipping even once might mean severed arteries, tendons, muscles. He could heal. Me, I might be crippled.

A surgeon would advise leaving it in so a pro could do it. Yeaaah, as if.

It was me, or nobody.

I leaned sideways, twisted my arms to get my hands closer, and found I had to zero in blindly while groping for the hilt. Rocking the knife back and forth seemed to slowly loosen it and I kept at it.

I paused for a second.

My legs dangled near his head and felt awfully vulnerable.

"Damn you, Wolfe. Your biting tendencies are making me nervous."

He didn't stir and I again tried levering at the knife. When it came loose, my palm nearly slipped down and slid along the blade.

"Fuck!" Panting, I jerked away.

Could I use the knife to cut off the leather cuffs?

Worth a try, but after a minute of maneuvering the knife at my back, I cursed and gave up.

Truth was, I either was frantic enough to risk slitting my wrists, or I trusted him to let me go once the Keppra levels lessened in his blood and he woke.

Guess I was trusting him.

Tsking, I surveyed the top of his head and that tousled nest of black hair. What a catch. He was snoring, probably as smelly as I was now, after all my exertions, and drool leaked from one corner of his mouth.

I remembered the garland of flowers he'd made me, how much he cared for Lily, the little talks we'd had about life, family, other stuff that'd just slipped into daily conversations. Then, last of all, I remembered that he'd known I was dosing him and he'd let me decide what I wanted.

"Wolfe, you're batshit crazy, but you're nice when you can think straight."

Not that I'd seen or signed a contract that'd said I wanted to be screwed with the biggest dildo thing since the last Saturn rocket took off.

That old instruction: *Don't do anything I wouldn't like*. Was that why, if he stopped breathing, I was going to attempt CPR by kneeing his chest and breathing into his drooly mouth?

"Hell no." I knew it wasn't the reason.

I didn't want to be responsible for killing this man. "And I like you," I murmured. "Especially the cute things you do."

At some point, Lily had arrived had lain on the floor in the middle of the room. She raised her head and eyed me.

"Am I right, girl?"

She ruffed and I laughed.

I slid off the counter, nearly dislocating my shoulder thanks to an unexpected topple backward, then I sat and nestled into Wolfe. He was going to be normal when he woke up, he was.

Had to be.

A moment later, Lily trotted over and curled up beside us.

"Complicated man," I murmured, as I closed my eyes. "God. I'm so thirsty."

CHAPTER 28

Wolfe

When I stirred, she was cuddled into me. Dried tears showed in tracks on her face. Her hair was sticking up every which way and tangled, and her cheek was squashed onto my arm, making her appear part orangutan. I patted her, blearily.

"Is okay. Fuck, I'm sorry, Kiara." I caressed her mouth, let my hand fall.

Waves of nothing swallowed me.

* * * * *

Blinking helped clear my eyes.

She was still here, in my arms, thank god.

I may have wept a moment. Not long enough for her to notice. Her eyes were opening.

"Did I say sorry?"

"Mmm. I think so." Her mouth twitched into a quick smile.

I got a smile?

I levered myself off the floor, and slowly stood, noticing my hand was free of the knife. "How?"

Grimacing, I stared at the neat hole. Blood decorated my arm.

Kiara tilted back her head then shrugged. "I got lucky. I jumped on the counter backward, knocked it loose."

What the hell? "You might've knifed yourself!"

Her second shrug only drew attention to her arms being behind her. She was still in the leather cuffs.

"Wait..." I coughed, cleared my throat of sludge. "There." I managed to get to the ladder minus any catastrophe, like falling.

Going down was even crazier. Blinking away the fogginess, I did it. Reached the bottom; found the keys.

Going up those stairs meant crawling.

I figured I'd given myself too much drug.

Figured, alright. I was a tad dumb.

I walked to her, dangling the keys and jingling them. "For the cuffs."

"You're back." She smiled. "I wondered what you were doing."

"Turn around."

Kiara swiveled on her knees, and for the first time since awakening, I really noticed she was naked.

Well. I was definitely slow. And, my cock was so sore. I'd probably done enough of that.

"Don't wriggle," I instructed, before leaning over her and unlocking the little padlocks.

While she was stretching her arms, I recalled some words she'd said earlier and snagged one of the bottles of drinking water off the counter. Then I threw myself down beside her and drew her to me. I unscrewed the cap.

"Drink."

She took a few good swallows, paused, then drank some more.

"I heard what you said before – that you were thirsty, and that I'm complicated."

She snorted and gave me the bottle. "Understatement of the year."

"Yeah." After drinking the rest, I set down the bottle. "Are we still good?"

Kiara sighed. "You're kidding?"

My heart dropped.

"Okay. Okay." Her hands pressed on her mouth for a second before she spoke. "I've had a lot of time to think this through. A real lot. You're a different man every time I turn around, Wolfe, but...I like bits from all of them. Except when you're totally absolutely bananas."

"Bits?"

She wriggled about and draped her arm over my chest. "Yes."

"Really?" I angled her head up so I could look into her eyes.

"You stabbed a knife into your hand. Why did you do that?"

"Uh huh." I sorted through my thoughts. "I decided I was going crazy again. That I needed more drug. Was the only way I could think of to stop myself. Save you, me. Needed time."

Her brow corrugated. "Time to make it work?"

"Yes."

"See. That's why."

She wasn't worried I'd do that again? "Why?"

"Vague question."

"Why are you trusting me?"

"Shut up. Later. Okay? I need to sleep." She mumbled, "Been watching you to make sure you didn't swallow your tongue for sooo long."

Her eyes closed and a sweet smile graced her mouth.

"Fine." I looked around. Kitchen floor? What did it matter? I snuggled in to keep her warm.

"'sides," she said softly. "You're nice, when you want to be. Like I said, I like you."

Ohhh, now. My heart did some maneuvers I never knew it could, flip-flopping. "Good," I whispered, and I kissed her forehead, gently. "Good."

Maybe, just maybe, I had hope.

Making her be with me was easy. Making her want to be, deep inside, in her heart, that was difficult, but I figured she'd just said something significant. I frowned. Though *nice* wasn't what I aimed for.

"And," she whispered. "You fuck like a god."

That made me grin.

CHAPTER 29

Kiara

We walked along what was now a familiar path. Our previous footsteps had bent the grass and made a flattened area to follow. It made this seem normal, as if we were a couple out for a picnic at a popular spot.

Wolfe carried a basket and a rug was slung over one shoulder. The sun shone through wisps of his hair where the wind flicked at them. That drew my eye, that and the shine on his biceps, the breadth of his shoulders under the light blue cotton shirt, and his sensual lips...those too. I guess I was a little besotted. Yeah, all that made him look like he was the god of fucking.

Though I'd said it jokingly, he'd not forgotten.

Twenty-four hours and we were off on a darn picnic.

I was still sore in so many places, though some of them gave me a happy tingle. His hand had a neat white bandage that needed changing later this afternoon. This morning, he'd taken his dose with me observing, after asking me how much was best.

When packing all the picnic food and gear, I'd asked why this, why today. He'd looked at me from under his brow and declared we needed to discuss things.

Things.

Where did one start with *things?* I glanced over at this man who prowled more than he walked, and at the small dog prancing at his feet. She'd dived on and squished a few grasshoppers and bugs on the way. The two of them together said everything.

I...liked the man who prowled, the man who wanted to discuss stuff, the man who made friends with small dogs.

His beast side scared me, but we could deal with that. But not with knives. I shuddered.

The field plateaued out a little and he halted, surveying the place as if it was new. I was pretty sure this was close to where I'd stood to shoot the revolver, and we'd had a picnic here before.

The creek gurgled below.

"Here will do." He unfolded the rug and flapped it out, letting it cloak the grass with its tartan kitsch.

The mundanity of us taking the plates, goblets, champagne, and tinned caviar and so on, from the basket made a nice contrast to how feral he made everything seem. I'd be struck by the strength in his hand, his fingers – in every detail – the tendons and the muscles of his neck, even the rugged crevices of his face.

He caught me looking more than once but said nothing.

When we were done, with a glass of champagne in hand he sprawled back onto his elbows and watched the sun-limned trees. Here had always been pretty and today it seemed brighter than ever, the blue flowers bluer, the yellow dandelions like dots of vivid paint bobbling in the breezes.

"It'd be freezing up here in winter." I took a sip of champagne, and rearranged the see-through chiffon at the bottom of my dress. It extended a foot past the mid-thigh hem of the white dress and made the garment seem naughtier than it really was.

Funny, how calm I felt.

"Yes. It would."

"The things you wanted to discuss?"

"Yes." He seemed lost in thought. "Are you staying with me, Kiara?"

"Oh. I have a choice?"

This moment was abruptly carved on the air.

I guess I knew of the potential for this to be discussed, but hadn't dared think it, not properly.

"Of course you do." Wolfe nodded, his eyes filled with a serene light blue.

"I thought..."

"I don't want to let you go. But I have to say this, offer it."

Have to. After all that had happened, asking me this was just some rule he'd decided on. Was I disposable? It miffed me. Which might be illogical. He was finally offering to free me, and I was feeling weird.

It was his matter-of-fact tone. "You seem calm. All this time spent making me stay —"

"I'm not..." He bit out. "Calm."

"Oh. Good." I swallowed. This was the big question and I should've studied for it like it was the exam to end all exams, but I hadn't. I'd avoided thinking about why I should stay. He hadn't seemed to allow choice.

But now he did.

And I found I couldn't imagine ever being away from him.

If I left and somehow, miraculously, assimilated back into the US work force, what would I do that wasn't like eating cardboard, *being* cardboard, compared to being with Wolfe?

Nothing, there was absolutely nothing to compare.

And neither of us had taken our eyes off the other while I'd thought this through.

Saying that out loud would seem insanity.

"Good," I repeated, licking my lips, delaying. "Because, I wouldn't stay with you, if I meant so little."

Stay, my mind was screaming, but I was still a little afraid, and so I was finding excuses.

"So. You're staying?" His hand arrived on my thigh and sneaked the chiffon out of the way. As always, a shock rippled into me at his touch. "Little? You don't mean little. You mean the world to me."

I shut my eyes to savor the sensation. Those words had tipped the balance.

Take a chance. Seize the day. Pick the harder, crazier option, for once in your life.

"Yes. I want to stay. I know it wouldn't make sense to anyone but us, but I want to be with you."

I chided myself. I'd forgotten something important to me but then, I couldn't see that I had much influence in that anymore.

"There's something else?"

His hand had stilled. Though he was being patient, it took me a moment to figure out what to say. "It's my parents — mother and step-father in Russia. I'm supposed to have brought you in.

Remember?"

"Yes. And we went through this. They probably think you're dead. Which is a pretty good excuse."

"I guess. I still worry. Like, if they see me alive and happy and with you."

"Then they'd have tracked us down and we'd have more to worry about than your parents. If, say, you leave me, how long before they find you anyway? Or the police?"

"Either way..." God, this was difficult to sort out. "They'd think you're controlling me?"

"Not if you're by yourself."

So, I was better off with him, and so was my family. In fact, if they found me again, alone, they might want me to do more things, more illegal things. At least if I was with Wolfe, we had a supernatural advantage.

This must be how a superhero's wife would feel. Safer with him than alone.

I would never be able to protect my parents from harm but being missing was better than being a blip on the radar of Russian intelligence again.

"Okay. Thanks. I feel better about that now."

"Good." His fingers traced circles on my skin. "I'd been in darkness for so long, since before I even met you, Kiara." The muscles of his jaw worked. "And only when I saw you, did the light return. That may sound dramatic, but it's true."

"Oh." That was so sweet. Tears filled my eyes but I refused to blink. I felt silly to be crying.

"It's just the truth." His hand was sensually caressing my thigh, but his mouth tweaked up at the corner. "I'm not a safe man to be with. I'd like you to be very, *very* sure. If this drug doesn't work —"

He was even going to knock me back, staying with him, if I didn't have the right attitude?

"It will." I squeezed my hand over his. "I'm a nurse. I can help. We can fine tune this."

"If we're wrong —"

I shook my head. "Won't be." God, I was digging myself a hole here, but I really didn't want to leave him. Not when it was my own choice. "We can figure out signs to recognize if you're going deeper."

"Hah. I can tell you one." His appreciative gaze slid over my front, my breasts, down to where his hand rested and the limits of the dress. "You gave me a dose like the last one, didn't you? I really want to fuck you right now."

"Shhh! Talking, remember? About things. Though, that is such a turn-on."

"Just saying it?"

I snorted in a most unladylike way. "Yes! Fuck you."

"Deal." His grin flashed out then faded. "That's my main sign."

"We need that one. I think most men would see that as normal."

"Yes." He squeezed my leg and shifted his hand under the dress. "I could drag this dress off you right now but, we have priorities. I need to be honest with you. No lies, no deceptions. I want this *right*."

"Okay." It reminded me of my own lies, at the beginning, of spying on him. I drew a breath then frowned. "You first."

"I still don't know my full name. You'd know if that's normal for people with amnesia?"

"It's not. Most recall who they are, but you're unusual, Wolfe, in a lot of ways. Maybe it'll come back. I don't think you should worry about it yet."

"Okay. And I have these memories that flash in. Bad ones."

Oh now. I knew that look. Veterans specialized in that stare. "Trauma does that. You know all about PTSD?"

"Yes." He nodded. "This is different, maybe. I see blood, terribly mutilated bodies. Dead people, underground. Women too, I think. It's very specific and very chilling."

"Any special reason why? These sorts of nightmares are common after being in battle."

"Why are they chilling? Because I feel I killed them all. A lot of people." He fastened his gaze on me. "Women especially."

Fuck, that was eerie.

What could I say? "I'm still not leaving you." I knew my forehead was wrinkling and that I didn't look confident. "I'm not a psychologist or a psychiatrist, but I know you."

"You've seen how bad I can get. I worry. *I* really don't know me. When I go deep, I forget what I do to you."

Could he do what he imagined in his nightmares while the beast? The answer was *possibly*.

It was also the past. I had such an investment in the man before me now. I would do whatever it took to keep him safe and sane. This was him, essentially, laying it all out on the table, and asking for my help.

Done. I would help him.

"But you're not going there anymore. Not going deep. I swear it. If nothing else, I can be your little private nurse. We can do this. All we need is a supply of the drug."

He nodded. "Yes."

"And the knowledge of the dose that works. Which we have...except." I smirked. It seemed a good time to distract him. "Maybe a little fiddling with it might be worthwhile. I like you dirty. I like you when you fuck like a god."

"Like? Only *like*?"

His contemplative expression had morphed slowly into one I knew well. Menacing yet exciting. Good but mean as fuck.

"You're trying to tempt me, little miss nurse."

His long intake of breath was accompanied by an examination of me that seemed likely to have discovered more than my last x-ray...and he could see into my mind when he wanted to.

"Never," I whispered.

"If only I had a latex nurse uniform." Wolfe used the base of his empty champagne glass to nudge the chiffon higher then he drawled out, "Spread your legs, and pull aside the crotch of your panties. If you're good..." His eyebrow tilted. "I might let you come, later. Much, *much* later."

Fuck fuckitty fuck.

How did he arouse me so fast? I swear my pulse was galloping and my clit swelling already. As I sat up on my knees and reached for the hem, I couldn't help the automatic response where my tongue played with my lips. I began to inch up the dress.

"Faster. Or I might find something to birch your ass with."

I squeezed shut my eyes, saying shakily, "You, sir, should be illegal."

He chuckled. "These need to feel the air too." I felt his hand on the low neck of the dress and he wriggled it down and scooped my breasts from the soft bra top I'd worn. "If anything, it's a crime not to display your tits."

"Breasts," I corrected. *Tits* was such an ick word.

"You're arguing with my label for your tits?"

I stared. I thought about debating this, but his expression seemed to threaten punishment. Exciting to wonder what that might be, but today I'd play his game. I added quietly, "No."

"Good." He inserted his finger under the crotch of my panties. "Play with your...tits." His finger cruised along my wet slit, barely grazing my pussy entrance, before he circled it. A few times he pushed on the hole enough that I knew a tiny amount of force would pierce me. "Play. Now."

With my eyelids fluttering from the pleasure, I put my hands up and cupped my breasts, and began to play, brushing my nipples with my thumbs. He had me panting within seconds, and opening my legs wider soon after, and he hadn't even stuck his finger in me.

"Keep going. I'm going to get you to slide that dirty little pussy down my cock when I can see you're wet enough."

"Oh god." I groaned. "Shut up."

He picked up my own half full glass and drained it while still playing absentmindedly with my slit. While I was sitting there before him, hands over my breasts, entirely enraptured, and attempting to not squirm on his finger. "Birching is now guaranteed."

This man would either end me or explode me with lust..

CHAPTER 30

Kiara

Wolfe was going down the mountain into town again. Daytime, but he'd become blasé about hiding his activity. I suppose the townspeople would dismiss him as some regular visitor? I wasn't sure if he intended to move on soon, but I suspected it.

Maybe I should ask.

When he stooped to kiss me, I kissed him back then grabbed his arm before he could go to the SUV.

At our feet, Lily whined. She knew he was leaving too.

"Take care of her while I'm gone. I should be back late this afternoon. Was there something you wanted to say?"

"Are we going somewhere else? I mean..." I shrugged. "I felt like you might be thinking that."

He looked off across the landscape beyond the cliff where it fell away past the cabin. "I don't know. We can't stay here forever, can we?"

"This place seems to have been deserted for years. We could use this as a base, go elsewhere, come back. We need to talk about the future."

Though the one thing we couldn't do was be normal, have friends, or invite the locals over. Or could we?

Maybe it was possible?

"Yeah. We'll talk some more about this. Later though." He kissed me again. "Take Lily for a walk."

"Alone? Like, by myself? You never let me leave the cabin much." How quaint, that'd shocked me.

"You're free now, remember? Go for a walk. Just take the gun and be careful. This is a mountain with wild animals. I left you a cellphone on the counter and my number's in there. If you do get lost, I can find you though. By feel."

I had a phone? I raised my eyebrows. "Seriously? By feel?"

The man was full of surprises.

"More so now than ever." He thumped his chest. "We're tied together. Here."

"Dayum," I whispered. "Awesome and creepy. All at once."

"That's me. Creepy." He walked backward a few steps, his hand emerging from his pocket with the keys. "When I come back I'm going to bend you over a tree stump and fuck you hard for saying that." He winked.

Just like him to leave me with my mouth open, and my mind churning through the sexy possibilities.

God, this was weird. Next, we'd be building that white picket fence around the cabin.

If we could keep him like this, the world was ours. *We.* Joint project. He was right; living on the edge of danger was a heady experience. I'd never before been this happy, excited, or even...satisfied. There was contentment in being such an integral part of someone else's life.

Did I deserve this?

I hung there, waiting to hear the crack of the mirror in which I lived, or the sound of someone turning the page of the fairytale book.

The noise from the engine faded and I woke myself.

"Okay, Lily. Walk it is. Please though, no dead creatures."

Why did dogs, even ones the size of a gnat, want to roll in dead things then trot into a house as if their smell alone wasn't biological warfare?

* * * * *

Damian

He lowered the binoculars. The small dust cloud stirred up by the SUV had settled.

"So. He is gone?" Guera lowered her own binoculars and rolled onto her side in the small observation post they'd set up above the cabin. "Shall we go find the woman?"

"Yes. We can either dispose of her, attempt to get her on our side..."

"Or?"

"One of those. I've run out of ideas." He rose to his knees, surveyed the surroundings then stood. "I doubt we can get her to cooperate, so we should kill her. It means less to worry about when we ambush him."

"No." Guera shook her head. "She's just a nurse. He won't be back for hours. You know that. We can try. We must try. We can restrain her if necessary. Killing her is not our objective. Am I getting soft?"

He laughed. "No. You're human. You're Guera. And I think you're right. It's not a flaw. Killing everyone we meet is not good. Besides, we might be able to frame her for the murder. Though having to drill a hole in his skull is going to make that difficult."

She was ignoring him, with her binoculars to her eyes. "We spoke too soon. A visitor is coming. Not Wolfe."

"Okay. Then we wait for them to go. We have days. There is no hurry."

"They are such beautiful love-birds. It will be a pity to spoil it."

"You know he's forcing her. It's not happiness if he's making her."

"Maybe." Guera sighed. "Maybe. You spoil the romance that I made up in my head. Anyway, we will wait." She grinned up at him. "You can always catch more Pokemon, hey?"

"There is that." He kneeled beside her and patted her ass. "And after watching that dirty pair fuck many times daily, I figure screwing you from behind while you keep an eye on the incoming visitor would be fine also."

"Oh my goodness."

But she didn't say no. So he reached under the waist of her khaki shorts, found the button and zip to her pants, and began to undo them. "How lucky that I have condoms."

Guera giggled but lifted her butt so he could get at the zip more easily. "Lucky? You are such a liar."

"Yes. I am well trained at deception."

"And at fucking, I hope. Be quick or I will lose interest and you'll have to do yourself."

For that comment, he leaned in and bit her plump bottom, until she made muffled squealing noises.

* * * * *

Kiara

We were half a mile of wandering track from the cabin, though less as the crow flies, when I heard a car coming up the road. It wasn't the SUV returning – I could tell from the sound. Since it passed us, I decided to pick up Lily and walk back. If they found the cabin and all the improvements, they might wonder who we were. And here was the flaw in our glittery future if we stayed. Not everyone was susceptible to Wolfe. Not men.

Though she tired quickly, Lily soon wriggled to be put down, so I set her on her feet.

She dashed off into the undergrowth and instantly became lost.

The unknown car, I had to leave it be while I searched for her – calling her name, cursing her, tramping through the forest and getting sticks in my socks and scratches on my legs.

Should've worn jeans, not denim shorts. One day I'd learn.

The road was to the left, down a bit of a slope, and I stepped around a dense copse of trees bounded by wildflowers, only to come face to face with a stranger.

He had Lily under his arm, a short gray beard, and a scruffy head of mostly gray hair. The cigarette in his mouth left a trail of smoke on the air. Distinctive, and I realized I hadn't smelled cigarette smoke for many weeks.

This then, was the world coming back.

"Hi there!" He dragged on the cigarette then pulled it from his mouth. "Found a dog. Yours? Lily? Heard you calling."

I nodded and held out my arms. When Lily wriggled, he set her down.

"Fucking cute thing." His wide grin wasn't just for the dog as his gaze very obviously tracked down my body.

I had the revolver at my waist, but my leather jacket mostly covered it. The gun made me feel safe, out here in the middle of nowhere, on a mountain with this stranger.

Funny, but I feared him more than Wolfe.

He was probably kind and sensible.

"Thanks." I bent to pat Lily and tried to calm the bouncing thing. Didn't work, but it gave me something to do. Asking this guy to have coffee, or something, might be polite but it wasn't happening. "What are you doing up here?"

"Ohh." He snorted phlegm then jerked his chin backward, in the direction of the cabin. "I heard gossip someone had squattered in the old cabin. Thought I'd take a look. It's been repossessed you know. I put in a bid to buy it."

"Oh?" I inclined my head.

"Yeah. I could let you have it. For a price."

"Really?"

"That is, if it is *you* with all the stuff at the cabin. You've been doing quite a bit of work!"

I twisted my lips. "I'll let my...husband, know."

"Sure. You do that. I'm a cool guy. Easy as pie to sell it back."

Lily was making excited dog sounds up the slope and he looked there and tossed his cigarette aside. "She's found you something? You're going to lose that critter again."

"A dead pigeon probably." I recalled the phone and dug in my pocket.

I let him wander off upslope while I rang Wolfe. He needed to know about this.

You okay? His voice sent a wave of relief through me. I was so reliant on this man.

"Yes, but we have a visitor. A man who says he's buying the cabin. He wants to sell it back though."

Damn. That'd mean signing things. We can't do that.

True.

"Will I get him to stay?"

No. Be safe though. I don't like him being there. Tell him your boyfriend is coming back soon. Because I am. I'll be a little longer than usual driving back. Had to use the north road as there's a bad landslide on the other and a big hole in the road. I nearly went over the side.

"Okay. Except, you're my husband."

He laughed. *Get rid of him. Tell him I'm coming.*

"Sure. Bye."

Bye.

I could hear the guy yelling something and I needed to see what he was up to. He didn't seem the type to hurt the dog, but...

When I reached where he stood, on a flat area under some trees, I found him shooing Lily away from a hole she'd dug, with his foot.

"Fuck. Man. We're gonna need the cops up here."

"What?" I stepped forward, frowning.

It wasn't difficult to see why he wanted the cops.

The recent storm must've loosened the soil here too. It had a little terraced, raised area and the earth had crumbled at the edge, exposing a two foot chunk of fresh dirt. Lily had only enlarged the mini landslide. In the freshly dug soil were bones. Human ones. I knew exactly what I looked at this time. No doubts. No possibility of doubts.

"Holy crap. Is that a bit of jewelry?"

"Yes." I clicked my fingers to call Lily away and, for once, she obeyed.

The amethyst bracelet from the photo was here. Purple stones glinted in the specks of sunlight filtering through the foliage. I kneeled and spotted the distinctive, gold heart half-buried in the soil. The bones were those of the wrist and hand – carpals, metacarpals, phalanges. Only, I gulped, there were more metacarpals than there were phalanges, and those were the finger bones.

I knew where the rest of the phalanges resided – at the cabin, in the lowest drawer by the bed, in a little cardboard box I'd found.

This was Amelia. She was dead.

The earth was cool and soft under my palm.

Unless someone had stolen her bracelet?

Whoever this was, someone had buried her here. Had Magnus killed her and hidden her body? For some reason her fingers had been cut off and burned in the fireplace.

Or crushed. The bones here, and those at the cabin, weren't cleanly cut.

Or...I froze...or chewed off.

Fuck.

I picked the bracelet out of the dirt, grimacing as bones fell away, ignoring the guy's comments about disturbing a crime scene. Already I had a notion, an evil, nauseously bad one that was making my heart rattle. While rubbing the dirt off the gold, I climbed to my feet.

"No cops."

"Why? Why no cops? Unless you're guilty of something?" With a superior grin on his ugly face and hands on hips, he spat out, "What the fuck are you telling me?"

Asshole.

"Go." I swiped back the jacket so he'd see the gun, put my hand on the butt. "Fuck off and go."

"Heyyy. No need for that, girlie. I'm going."

I watched him stumble down the slope. He must've thought he was safe because he yelled out, "You watch yourself! Cops will be here soon!"

Fuck him. I fumed. An idea clicked into place. It would slow him down, if nothing else. If he took the bait.

"My husband is coming back up the north road *right now*. I phoned him. You wait! He'll be on you, mister!"

I pulled out the gun and fired a shot in the air.

He ran. He ran like hell, and a few minutes later I watched his car tear down the road. I was pretty sure he didn't take the north road, though he must've come up that way. What a putz.

Maybe I was a little nasty and a lot hasty, but I had worse things to worry about. Someone in the past had killed Amelia. Maybe bitten off her fingers then burned them.

If it was just some ancient killing, it was tragic and sad, but not terribly relevant.

Except...I guess I had this hunch. Which was why I kept cleaning off that heart, rubbing away the grime over the engraving on the back.

Once I shone it up with my thumb and some spit, what I saw there made my stomach churn. Bile spilled into my throat.

With love, from Magnus W.

There hadn't been room to engrave his full name.

It might be Williams or Wood or any number of W names.

Might be...

Or Wolfe.

I squatted and stared at the grave, thinking, or trying to, but it was hard to do that when I felt so sick. I might've sat there for ten or twenty minutes.

What if Wolfe had done this?

Was it such a surprise?

No. Not really. He wouldn't remember it, if he had.

I should do something.

I rose to my feet, though my body felt empty with a frigid wind whistling through me, pushing me off balance.

Something cold and hard, and made of metal, pressed on my temple.

"Do not move, Miss. This is a Glock at your head. A gun that can easily blow your brain out the other side of your skull. Raise your hands." A man's voice. I raised my hands, trembling. "I will take your gun and then we will go somewhere to talk. Be good and you will not be hurt. Okay?"

I felt someone's hand at my waist remove the revolver. When they stepped away and the gun remained at my temple, I knew there were two of them.

They'd been so silent. Like fucking ninjas. It was a clue. I figured these were professional hunters. My Russian colleagues.

I swallowed. "Okay."

"Good."

CHAPTER 31

Kiara

They took me a few hundred yards up the mountain, to a hideout inside a thicket of trees and shrubs. From here I could see downslope and even glimpse the roads in places, where they wound upward and the trees had been cleared.

An observation place, a hide.

How long had they been watching us?

The zip-ties at my wrists were impossible to break, but then I guess they knew that.

"Put your ankles together, Kiara."

The woman kneeled a yard away, waiting.

I obeyed as I couldn't see the point in the opposite. They both had guns and I was sure could take me down in a fight in one second, flat.

Her man trained his Glock on me while she circled each of my ankles, linked them, and adjusted the fit. Great. No running. Not that I could out-sprint a bullet.

They'd found Lily and leashed her with rope. She lay near my feet, watching us, her ears twitching whenever he talked.

Wolfe was coming back, and I couldn't warn him.

But he was a murderer, wasn't he?

"Hello, Miss Kiara," the man said. "You know who we are? You were supposed to hand Mister Wolfe over to us."

I nodded, not trusting myself to speak. If they asked me more about Wolfe, I wasn't sure I could speak of him. I could *feel* this potential roadblock.

The male accomplice was a slightly balding, lean man of average height, average looks really. Nondescript was probably best for their line of work. Though the woman was quite beautiful. Her white hair set off her perfect bone structure.

"You may call me Z, just so we have a label. My partner, she can be A." He made himself comfortable, leaning on a crooked tree trunk, with the gun drooping and pointing to the right. "Why didn't you?"

I raised my eyebrows.

"We expect you to talk. If you don't, you know things will happen to your family. Yes?"

Oh god.

"You know we know of Wolfe's powers? That he can make you do things. Hmm?"

The roadblock evaporated. His simple words, telling me he knew, seemed to have accomplished that. I cleared my throat.

And yet, I didn't want to betray Wolfe. I frowned at the dirt before Z. Why?

"You know also his full name?"

I jerked my head up and stared at him. Was he –

"His name is Magnus Wolfe."

Oh hell. Then he'd owned the cabin in the past. Amelia had been his. The bracelet, he'd given her that, taken the photos, and probably killed her. That terrible thing he'd written of would be him killing her?

Surely he was evil?

I raised my head and found Z and A staring back.

"What?" He leaned forward. "Did that come as a shock? Why?"

I bit my lips. If I told them things, maybe my family would be okay. I could. Wolfe had said I was free. There was nothing, at all, stopping me.

"I didn't know his name," I croaked. "That's who first owned the cabin."

"Oh? The cabin's old owner was not supposed to be Magnus Wolfe, but that is interesting. The body down there." He twitched the gun. "The skeleton. Do you know who that was?"

Squeezing my eyes shut, I tried to think. Would this hurt Wolfe?

If it did, I'd feel bad.

Tears filled my closed eyes. Stupid. He'd killed.

Not a surprise. Maybe that was why I wasn't reacting as I should be.

The writing he'd done, what he'd said, what if that was when he first became who he was now?

That revelation ticked in, cogwheels turned. It fitted. He'd forgotten being Magnus, wouldn't even remember anything from then, except that he'd once stayed here.

That was the truth.

I'd forgiven his beast behavior before. This didn't change that.

And telling Z some of this might help my cause. "What..." I swallowed. "Do you intend to do to Wolfe?"

The woman spoke. "We'll be killing him. He was a subject in a research trial in Thailand – an experiment that escaped. The locals thought he was a monster who ate people. He is not very nice man, Kiara. We need a sample of his brain tissue. You will die too, if you don't co-operate."

Crap. And a row of fucks.

That history added a whole other layer to Wolfe and I couldn't sort it out now. Poor man. What could I *do*?

"Does he have weapons? Can he fight? Did you tell him about us? And who is the buried person?"

I rocked back and forth a tiny amount. Helping Wolfe would hinge on yelling at the right time, to warn him. What I said now probably would do nothing, either way. Lying a little *might* help.

"She was a woman called Amelia, I think. A friend of Magnus, long ago. I don't think he remembers her."

"Do you know how she died?" Z asked.

"Not really." I sucked in a breath then went on. "Wolfe has a gun, yes. He's good with it. Very good. He's big and can fight as far as I know."

They both shrugged.

Scaring them wouldn't be easy, but they might be warier. They wanted a god-damned brain tissue sample? That was diabolical and somehow worse than merely killing.

I lowered my voice to a menacing level. Or tried to. "He knows about you."

"Hmmm. This phone..." He had turned on my cellphone. "No

password, good. He's in the town?"

I nodded, feeling the lie screw into my chest. I had an aversion to lying.

He's coming here, you asshole.

"Good. I will text him and tell him to return from the town because you have lost the dog." He flashed me a smile. "We have seen how you both love Lily."

He tapped in the message. Not long after sending it, the cellphone signaled a return text.

"I am coming ASAP. Will be an hour and a half. Be careful. I will find you." Z smiled. "Hook, line, and sinker."

Wolfe knew something was wrong. I nearly smiled too but wrestled my mouth into a glum line.

"Now then, Guera, what else should we ask her?"

"First," she said, from under her brow. "We don't say our names."

Z only grunted.

That was when I was sure he meant to kill me. I tugged at the ties, in vain, but it made me feel productive. I glanced at Lily who was now snoring. If only she was a trained attack dog, I'd have her rip their throats out.

"You know," I began in a whisper, having remembered something vital. Could I make them leave by saying this?

But they'd still kill me. Now I knew what fatalism was. If they left, at least Magnus might escape.

"What? Useless." He was still looking at my cellphone. "You don't have Pokémon on this?" He placed it on his thigh. "What is it?"

"The cops will be here soon. I chased a man away with my gun. He's gone to get them."

"Pfft." Guera puffed out her lips. "No. Don't you worry about him. They aren't coming."

How could she know this? I switched my gaze from one of them to the other, and back. "What?"

"They aren't coming. Tell me about Wolfe's powers. How he makes you fuck him. I wouldn't mind that one." Z stood and came to me, looked down.

"Stop intimidating her. She's nice. I don't like threats. You know that."

He looked back at Guera. "On this you are wrong. I think she's being reticent and lying."

Then he whipped around and smashed the flat of his hand across my face. While I recovered, gasping and feeling the sting throbbing into my cheekbone, he squatted beside me, shifting his feet to get comfortable.

"I don't like threats either, but sometimes we need them. Understand? Tell me something good about him. Something that helps us. Otherwise you will die in great pain."

He trailed the muzzle of the gun across my breasts, pressing the T-shirt into my nipples and miming *bang, bang.*

Jesus. Eyes wide, I found I couldn't stop looking at him.

I spewed information.

I told him my theory about Wolfe murdering Amelia. It made him excited about the possibility of framing Wolfe for any murders they did. I kept talking, blurting out stuff that they probably didn't need to know, talking louder, more panicky. Definitely louder. Deliberately so.

Z smacked me again, rocking my head sideways. "Not so crazy!"

Blinking away tears, I stayed quiet because, minutes ago, I'd felt a presence.

Wolfe.

Just as Wolfe had said he could find me by feel, I could feel him. He was nearby and coming closer. A man who had murdered, but I believed in who he was *now.* That was what mattered.

I strained to hear but there was nothing that said a man was out there.

Nothing.

Lily kept on snoring in gentle bursts.

Maybe that was why I couldn't hear him. He wouldn't be armed, unless he had a gun I'd not seen. Him against these two professional killers.

Nothing out there...

Until Guera rose and looked around, with her gun in her hand.

Z stood too. "What is it?"

"A noise?" She pointed toward the peak of the mountain, higher upslope, and my throat squeezed in, my blood pounding in my temples.

My hands were sweating but the slickness didn't let me slip them loose from the ties.

"There," she repeated softly.

Z made a hand signal and crouched, moving aside a branch, as if to worm his way out of the hide.

And Guera slammed her gun into the back of his head and ripped his weapon from his hand as he sprawled in the dirt. "Don't move," she spat.

The branches behind me crackled and rustled. Shadows wavered. Wolfe stepped into the hide, filling the space with his bulk.

"Mine." He put out his hand and Guera tossed the Glock to him then went back to guarding Z, who was on his hands and knees, groaning. "Thank you, Guera. I didn't catch most of the conversation. What's his name?"

"Damian." There was a trapped look in her eyes. I knew it well. She'd be feeling confused, scared, and maybe turned on. Wolfe had that effect.

If he tried to fuck her, I would kill him.

"I won't," he whispered in an aside. Then he said, louder, "A knife? Please. So I can cut Kiara loose."

Without fanfare, Guera slipped a knife from a waist sheath and threw it over. It landed point first in the log, a few inches from where I sat, and stood there quivering.

"Tie him up. Hands and feet, and hogtie him too, please."

All these *pleases*, as if we were guests at a dinner party.

By the time my wrists and ankles were free, Damian was not.

"What are you going to do with them? They were going to kill you, and me."

"I don't know, yet." His lip curled. "Are they your associates?"

"Yes. I'm sorry."

"It's okay." He squeezed my shoulder. "We're going to have to leave, after all. The question is, do we leave two dead people or two live ones behind us?"

"It depends," I said, slowly. "On whether you want to be a murderer or not."

A loaded question.

I looked at Guera and Damian. One furious and tied up, the other sad, with her mind in a muddle and under Wolfe's control. "Both of them must have killed before."

"Meaning?" He gave me a thoughtful look.

"Maybe it would do the world a favor to kill them..." I let that fall away.

Where had that come from? I was a nurse, a saver of people. It'd come, I realized, from that investment I had in Wolfe. I'd rather they die than him.

"Which would be best for my family?"

"Hmmm."

"Also," I let my forehead wrinkle up. "That visitor I had. I made him angry and he said he'd fetch the cops, but these two said it wasn't a concern."

I'd sent him down the landslide road. Had they seen something happen?

"So many questions. Keep him here, Guera. We'll be back." Wolfe took my hand and led me out of the hide. "I'm taking you back to the cabin."

"But..." I almost skipped backward. "What about them?"

"They aren't going anywhere. The walk will let me figure out what to do with them. And whatever I do, you're not going to be here when I do it."

"Oh."

The firm set to his mouth and tone of his voice said either justice or vengeance was on his mind. I held his hand more firmly. "Okay. Whatever you decide, I believe in you."

"Good. Because I heard you call me Magnus Wolfe." He stopped and turned to me. "How long have you known?"

"Today. I swear." My mouth trembled. "I wouldn't lie."

"I know. Come."

Then he stalked onward.

When we reached the cabin, I thought he would tell me to quickly pack whatever we might need but instead he took me down to the basement and collared me then leashed me to a point on the wall.

This wasn't freedom, but I dared not ask his reason. He was angry, and perhaps didn't know why. They'd said he might've eaten people. Which was so fucked up.

"Magnus Wolfe?" he said again.

"Yes." Though there seemed more to that question than name verification.

"I'll be back, soon."

I hoped so, though I was afraid. I had lied to him by omission and then again by swearing I wouldn't lie. I hadn't told him everything, especially not about Amelia or my suspicions, or the rumors about what might have happened to him in Thailand.

Wolfe wasn't normal, and I'd known that, but I did believe in him.

I'd been afraid he might kill me, because the potential was there when he sank deep into his crazy animalistic phase. Now I knew he'd killed a woman. *Nothing* had altered. The risk had always been there if the drug failed.

And I'd already accepted that.

He might kill me, one day. I could either cut loose from him, when I had the opportunity, or I could stay with him, help him be the good man that he was when sane, and pray like mad that he never became that animalistic again.

Yeah. I nodded and took a calming breath then sat on the rug, arranging the chain leash so it didn't pull on my neck. Beneath the rug was hard, cold floor.

I would wait for him, in good faith.

CHAPTER 32

Wolfe

Chaining her to the wall was rough after saying she was free. I didn't care. I'd wanted to do it – better than shaking her until she fessed up. She was lying to me, in some way. She was lying.

That was all I could think as I retraced my steps to where the two Russians waited.

I had to determine their fate, based not on what was good for them, but on what was good for me and Kiara.

That was the key. What was good for us both.

I paused to rub my forehead.

I cared for her so much that a lie should be allowable. I hated the idea of forcing her to say what she'd lie about. Either she would tell me, or she wouldn't.

I'd chained her up because I was angry. Everyone got angry at their partner at some point. Everyone lied too. Honesty was a hard gig to follow.

When I ducked and pushed aside the branches so I could enter the hide, the answer hit me.

Whatever I did to these two, I might not tell Kiara the truth about it either. Or not all of it.

And I would be doing that so as not to hurt her. She wouldn't like me killing them.

A lie could sometimes be the best choice. Perhaps her lie was for my benefit.

Yes. That was it.

With my anger lessened, I could now judge what to do.

I sat on Kiara's log and beckoned Guera over. "Bring more of those zip ties."

A strong-willed woman – new to this, she was wriggling in her head, trying to shake me loose.

"You can't do it," I said, gesturing for her to kneel facing away from me. "I can control you like a puppet. "Didn't you two know this? I mean...Russia wants me? It has to be because of this?"

"Yes," she croaked out. "It is. We knew. They don't have all the facts but they think you were a CIA agent, once. We thought I could stay out of range."

"Wrong."

Me? CIA? And my name was Magnus Wolfe.

I rolled that around, saying it in my mind. It sounded right and good. Yet shocking too. CIA?

Jesus H.

This was like the tooth fairy delivering unexpected presents but pulling a few extra teeth because she wanted to. Good teeth. I wasn't sure who I was anymore.

"Not many women can resist what I do." I finished the wrist tie and started on her ankles.

Then I dragged her over to her hog-tied partner, the silent one who glared. I double-checked his bonds.

Though I wasn't one hundred percent sure of what I'd do with them, I'd had a fair bit of time to think on the way over.

"Start with this police thing," I instructed Guera. "What's that about?"

"Your woman fired a shot and argued with a man about something. There's an old skeleton, a grave site your dog found, and the man saw it too. He drove off erratically and we watched him from here. If you know where to look, you can see the gash where his car left the road."

"He crashed? At a fresh landslide?"

"Yes."

"So, you didn't shoot him or anything? With a sniper rifle?" I gestured at a few long bags lying around. At least one looked to hold a rifle.

"No. The shot would be impossible."

"He's just a bad driver," Damian added. "Stop messing with us."

"Messing?" I snarled out. "After you bruised Kiara's face and threatened to kill us both? I'll mess if I want to."

Damn him.

"What were you two going to do with me?"

The man clamped his mouth into a line.

Guera however... "Kill you and obtain a sample of your brain tissue."

"Uh huh. Woohoo. Nice. A pair of murderers."

So was I, if my nightmares were based on reality.

The rangers here would notice the landslide. There'd be people crawling everywhere soon in any case. We had to get out of here. They'd find the man's car. This was going to cause a fuss. These two though?

If I killed them, their superiors would likely figure out Kiara was around still, and with me, and alive. There'd be DNA evidence all over the cabin and the cops were already after us. That might result in harm coming to her family.

If they thought she was dead, that'd be better. Arranging that sort of subterfuge would be near impossible and we had to leave here ASAP. There wasn't time for fanciness.

If I killed these two, their bodies might be found, in a year, a decade.

If alive, they were sneaky enough to work out how to get out of the zip-ties. Though it'd take them time.

Guera could testify to her superiors as to how I could make a woman do anything. That might help Kiara's family...except they'd seen her act like a free woman, without me around too. I needed to do something to make them see she wasn't free, even if she was. That she was a victim too, even if she wasn't, anymore.

I needed to make the danger very real.

"Well." I rubbed my chin. "Seems like I have to do something you two won't like. Just to show you I mean business." I rose, with the hunting knife in hand – the knife I'd used to cut Kiara's ties. "I'll make it quick, but it won't be painless. This is what I do to people who disobey me or try to hurt me or Kiara. Or just annoy the fuck out of me. Kiara is mine, my property."

I tested the blade on my thumb. Sharp enough to cut air.
Funny how you got used to people screaming.

CHAPTER 33

CIA, Langley

Hardinger noted the email coming in and the high priority, logged on, and read.

Hardinger. Your eyes only.

Please decide on further action.
Request from NYPD for DNA identification of a tissue sample from the alleged Andy Carruthers. Sample has been found identical to the DNA of Magnus Wolfe, a previous CIA operative, seconded to aid in a high security research project in Thailand eleven years ago. Details of this research are no longer available.

Wolfe was suspected of involvement in the disappearance and possible murder of his wife, Amelia Wolfe. For undisclosed reasons, the subject was allowed to leave the USA to participate in the research project.

Magnus Wolfe had been declared missing, presumed dead.

Facial recognition from provided photographs also confirms with a 95.6 % probability that this is Magnus Wolfe.

Subject therefore confirmed as Magnus Wolfe.

He is believed to be currently in the USA and is sought in relation to alleged kidnapping, assault, sexual assault, and various vehicular charges.

Hardinger made his chair squeak as he thought, rotating it a fraction of an inch this way, a fraction in reverse.

No matter how secret the project, this Wolfe should be apprehended. Who could he put on this?

The request by local law enforcement would be denied, of course. He accessed the file of available agents and began to scan them.

CHAPTER 34

Kiara

Waiting was scarier than knowing. I didn't want him to kill them, no matter how bad they were. I didn't know how angry he was at me, but I'd sensed I was partly his target.

The wall under my shoulder was cold and I leaned my forehead into it, letting the cold penetrate and wake me with the icy shock. I couldn't run from him and I still didn't want to.

When I heard him come in the door, then watched him descend the spiral staircase, tears of relief sprang into my eyes. I didn't care what he meant to do; I just needed to see him alive and well.

"Don't ask," he growled as he came to me. "I won't tell you."

About the Russians? That was all he thought of? "Are you angry at me?"

He unclipped the chain, gathered it and tucked it into his pocket. "I was. I came to see how things should be between us. We can be normal, as a couple. I'll leave you your secrets, if you leave me mine."

"Normal?" I smirked at the tail end of the chain he was shoving back in his jacket pocket.

"Yeah." His grin was good to see. Then it faded and the look he

192

gave me stirred me again to fear.

"What is it? We have to leave now? I know that."

There was something else. His forehead settled into a frown as he picked up my hand and smoothed his thumb over the backs of my fingers.

"I have to do something to you." He locked eyes with me. "It's necessary to make your Russian friends believe you're my victim and not my friend. Will you trust me?"

My heart was doing a frantic knock against my ribs. This was *bad* with many exclamation marks, I could tell, feel it.

I gulped down the fear. "I will. Now tell me."

"I think I will need your nurse skills. Yes..." He sniffed, cleared his throat. "We have to be fast but I want to be safe. Tell me what to get, what to use to help you afterward. Just this...I think I can take some of your pain."

"Pain?" I stared.

"I'm going to cut off one of your fingers and leave it here."

Fuck.

"What about just blood?" Say yes to that, for fuck's sake.

"It won't be enough. Not unless you lose some life-threatening amount." His mouth twisted into a grimace. "An ear might do, but I don't want to disfigure you that way."

An ear...and here I was choosing which. He was right though, I decided, sickeningly. A part of a finger would convince them he was a mean, fucked up man who hurt me just...because...he wanted to. I flexed the fingers he held. Which?

Get it over with.

He could take some of my pain? If that were so, I could do this.

Wolfe took a knife from the sheath at his waist. Guera's perhaps? I didn't recognize it.

A knife would be best. If clean.

My heartbeat counted out the seconds while I summoned some calmness.

"Okay." I thought furiously, pretending this wasn't for me. I stared up at the ceiling while I rattled off my ideas. "Get bandages, something to use for a small tourniquet, you should sterilize the knife in fire, if you can. Faster than boiling water, I guess. Maybe tie my hand down somehow, so I don't jerk away."

This was going to hurt like fuck. Wolfe took my left hand pinky in finger and thumb. "This one?"

I nodded and swallowed back rising bile. Best not to take a more useful digit. "At the joint but not just the tip as that'll look suspiciously nice." *Haha.*

"Hmmm. Okay."

"Pull back the skin toward my hand, really tight. See if you can leave some skin that can be stapled or stitched. Try not to cut bone. That'd make a mess."

Not like Amelia. I laid my head on his arm. "And be quick."

"I will." He stroked my hair. "Should I clean your skin with iodine? I have some."

Now that would really look odd to forensics. "No. We'll have to trust to antibiotics, afterward." And find a doctor to fix the mess.

And so it was done. He left me to gather everything and when he returned, serenity cloaked me. It was him, helping me. I surely didn't mind. When he laid the knife across my finger, I shut my eyes.

Thank god, he was right. He did take some of the pain. Into himself, I guessed, though I was too busy sobbing to see what effect it had on him. I wasn't numb, but I could stand the pain.

There was blood everywhere.

As a nurse, I should've been able to handle that. Seeing it was my blood splattered on the rug, on him, on me, and that was my finger lying on the floor – no. While he applied the tourniquet, I threw up, copiously.

If he'd tourniqueted it before cutting that would've looked odd to the cops too.

There wasn't time or the materials to stitch the wound. I'd have to make do with a bandage after the tourniquet came off. There was something very wrong about seeing a part of yourself missing.

"Kiara," Wolfe said in the swaying distance. "Tell me how to bandage this. Now! Do not faint."

His presence splashed into me like fire and ice. I jerked my head up. "Okay. Umm. Sure."

We managed.

Wolfe gathered our gear, what he could find and load quickly, and we drove off with me cradling my bandaged hand and applying pressure when the bleeding started again. At the last, the stump had gone numb.

Wolfe was better than a local anesthetic.

God, I'd left a finger back there.

"This had better be one time only," I muttered.

Wolfe chuckled. "Of course."

Partway down, I glimpsed the landslide through a cutting. It truly was massive and a ranger's vehicle was parked at the bottom. Lower down the slope, though beyond where they could see easily, was a smashed vehicle. It must've been heading down the mountain when it crashed, from the looks of it.

The visitor. Had the Russians observed the accident? I figured that was why they knew he wasn't returning with cops.

There was no regret in my heart. No sadness. Maybe too much violence had happened today? Maybe my soul was numb at the moment. Or maybe, I was becoming hardened to the idea that sometimes you had to sacrifice others if you wanted to live life your way.

Bad things happened. Best if they happened to others.

CHAPTER 35

Wolfe

I could hear Lily snoring in the back seat. The dog had a switch that let her sleep anywhere, anytime.

Kiara was quiet now, and lay with her head on my thigh, rocking as the SUV went over rough spots on the road. The handbrake must've been digging into her side even with my jacket cushioning it.

"You should have your seatbelt on, and be sitting up." I murmured. "It's safer."

"Not now, please. I need to touch you. It helps."

"Okay." I reached down and caressed her head, feeling her soft hair shift. "I love feeling you too."

Her amused snort was unexpected.

I shook my head, smiling. "Wasn't meant to be dirty."

"Suuure it wasn't."

"Though come to think of it, you're a few inches away from a blowjob."

"Hmmm." Her breath warmed my skin through the denim. "Maybe later."

"Good to know."

"I'm serious. Strangely. It'd take my mind off this." She raised her bandaged hand.

Even now the blood made me scowl. "I'm sorry. Sorry we had to do that, Kiara."

Her sigh was long. "Me too."

"The painkiller helping any?"

"A little. Though you're the best painkiller." She turned onto her back and kissed my palm.

I nodded, feeling blessed that I could help her.

"I found some wildflowers for you, on the way down the mountain earlier."

"That's so sweet," she said, her voice husky.

"Really?"

Tears shone in her eyes.

I steered us around one of the long curves that led down the mountain.

"Guess I'm feeling fragile." She sniffed and I glimpsed her wiping her eyes.

"That's okay. I'd kiss you better if I could. The flowers. They're in the glove box."

"You picked some? Wow." She sat up and opened the glove compartment. "Awww. Pretty."

"Just some bluebells and some red flower I don't know the name of. Hope they're not poisonous." I grinned as she put the small ragged bunch to her nose.

"They smell nice too. You're a gorgeous man."

"I can be." I patted my thigh. "Lie down again."

Her look said she liked both the idea and that I wanted her there. When she was again lying with her head on my thigh, I ran my finger under the black collar I'd left on her.

"You going to take that off?"

"You can wear it a bit longer. I like it on you."

"Mmm. I guess. I don't mind."

I resumed patting her.

We'd get there. Find our way. I had plans for leaving the USA. We'd work our way down south and once on the coast, I had memories that told me how to work the system and get onto a boat without being stopped.

Thailand?

Wasn't sure I wanted to go there again, even if it might clear up my past.

I'd talk it over with Kiara and figure this out.

I had this vision of us being married under the sun of a tropical country, confetti raining down, and people smiling and generally being happy. That was going to happen. I would make it so. The more I found out about myself, the more confident I was of this power.

I steered around another long corner then flexed my fingers into the leather steering wheel cover. My strength reassured me.

We could do this.

We had a good future coming.

I wondered if to Kiara this was her *twu love*. For me, I figured it was.

"The pain coming back?" I could feel the twinge. "Need me to take it away?"

Sleepily she murmured a *no*. Stubborn girl. I kissed my hand then applied it to her cheek. "Have a second-hand kiss."

"Mmm."

She was falling asleep. It'd been a very big day.

The pain taking away thing...

I remembered.

I'd done it with Guera too. Not all the way as I figured they both needed to feel pain – seeing they deserved it. They'd hurt Kiara, meant to kill me. Assholes. Even if it was their job.

They were in love, though. It was part of why I hadn't done more.

I'd carved a *W* into the man's back.

Like I'd decided, Kiara didn't need to know. Only that I hadn't killed them.

Guera...

The ziplock plastic bag was in my jacket pocket, the one next to the door.

Four fingers.

I'd taken *some* of her pain.

I should probably throw those away when Kiara was asleep.

Something had compelled me to keep them.

Wouldn't hurt to hang onto them for a while longer. I was curious about my reason. Always good to know why I did things. My past was such a fucking mystery.

CHAPTER 36

Kiara
Three months later. Cuba.

For two foreigners getting married in Havana, Cuba, we'd done well. Though we couldn't have a full church wedding, due to our needs for secrecy, or indeed a true civil marriage for the same reasons, Wolfe had done us proud.

The walls had lost their original color, flaked away by years of the elements. The ornate curled decorations, the baroque architecture, the wrought iron – all gave this location a delicious flavor of decadence and history.

We'd arrived here weeks ago. The go-fast boat, as they called it, that'd brought us from Florida to Cuban soil had been the simplest part of our journey. Normally they took Cubans to US soil, or maybe drugs.

We were in the courtyard of a crumbling Spanish colonial house owned by a cousin of the owner of our *casa particular* – Karel. Or maybe a cousin of a cousin. It had been an exuberant gesture of his to sort this out for us. He'd been aghast at our lack of celebration, as had his wife, Athena.

Was it natural or Wolfe's doing? Athena had no doubt had much to do with this.

They were some of the friendliest people I'd ever met, but... Wolfe had perfected a subtle control method so I could no longer tell what he'd made happen and what came naturally.

With the encouragement of Karel and his young wife, a local band had materialized too, along with chairs, tables, and a supply of alcohol and food. We were paying for this, but prices here were so low it'd barely make a dent in our cash.

The chance to participate in an impromptu reception cross party had seemed infectious.

"Here. Let me get some of this from your hair, beautiful one." Wolfe's murmur from behind me, with his mouth inches away and his breath stirring the small hairs on my nape...as always, I shivered.

When he began picking the white confetti from my hair, I turned in his arms, only to receive a soft kiss on my lips.

The twenty or so Cubans, who were friends of Karel, cheered and I couldn't help smiling over Wolfe's shoulder at them. They thought we'd had a civil ceremony earlier, though really all we could do was say our vows to each other while standing in the light waves of the beach.

The water had been glass when it stilled before the next wave, and tiny fish had flitted past our legs.

"I love you and will be yours forever," had been the gist of our vows. It was more than enough for us. We'd wanted something to formalize our relationship.

Maybe one day we'd reach a country where we felt safe to register our marriage under our true names.

"More mojitos!" sang Karel, raising his glass. "For the bride and groom, Cedro, por favor!"

Wolfe held me at arm's length. "Or champagne?"

"Mojitos will do. Then..." I pressed my forefinger on the button of his white dress shirt and admired the look of his suspenders. The Panama hat had gone missing, thank god. I wasn't sure he suited one. "*Then.*" I peeked from under my brow. "We shall try to dance the salsa?"

"Hmmm. Is this to be your means of torturing me?"

I looked to Karel. "Your promise? To teach us to dance the salsa. Is that still on?"

"Of course! Music!" He raised his arms dramatically.

Wolfe rolled his eyes and gave a majestic sigh. "For this, at midnight I will dunk you in the ocean..." He pulled me closer and whispered, "Naked."

I smirked. If he dared. The indecency laws here might mean he'd get us arrested.

"How about the bath tub?"

"That depends... On what you do." He waggled his eyebrows.

"Oh." I touched my tongue to my teeth, thinking... Or what he made me do.

The unexpected was often best.

"As you wish." I smiled as I said those words from *The Princess Bride*. Anticipation peaked my nipples. Luckily, the embroidery and beads on the bodice hid such body signs. "How long are we staying here, in Cuba?"

"Forever, if my twu love wishes it so."

My smile grew as he wrapped his hand over mine – with reverence where he touched my shortened finger – and his other hand cupped my waist.

In this moment, forever seemed good.

"Shall we dance?" Wolfe's blue eyes took on a feral amusement. "Before I decide you're too tasty to leave uneaten."

It was my turn to roll my eyes.

"I have a confession to make, Kiara. I already know how to dance."

The trumpets, guitars, and bongos began to play. Before Karel could reach us, Wolfe swept us across the floor, and Cuba's music twirled us into her arms and into her heart.

ABOUT CARI SILVERWOOD

Cari Silverwood is a New York Times and USA Today bestselling writer of kinky darkness or sometimes of dark kinkiness, depending on her moods and the amount of time she's spent staring into the night.

When others are writing bad men doing bad things, you may find her writing good men who accidentally on purpose fall into the abyss and come out with their morals twisted in knots.

If you'd like to learn more or join my mailing list go to www.carisilverwood.net
Also Facebook & Goodreads:
http://www.facebook.com/cari.silverwood
http://www.goodreads.com/author/show/4912047.Cari_Silverwood

You're welcome to join this group on facebook to discuss Cari Silverwood's books:
https://www.facebook.com/groups/864034900283067/

Also by Cari Silverwood

Dark hearts Series
(Dark erotic fiction)
Wicked Ways
Wicked Weapon
Wicked Hunt

Pierced Hearts Series
(Dark erotic fiction)
Take me, Break me
Klaus
Bind and Keep me
Make me Yours Evermore
Seize me From Darkness
Yield

Preyfinders Series
(Erotic scifi)
Precious Sacrifice
Intimidator
Defiler
Preyfinders – The Trilogy

Preyfinders Universe
Cyberella

Squirm Files Series
(Parodies of erotic romance)
Squirm – virgin captive of the billionaire biker tentacle monster
Strum – virgin captive of the billionaire demon rock star monster
The Well-hung Gun – virgin captive of the billionaire were-squid gunslinger monster
The Squirm Files anthology

The Badass Brats Series
The Dom with a Safeword
The Dom on the Naughty List
The Dom with the Perfect Brats
The Dom with the Clever Tongue

The Steamwork Chronicles Series
Iron Dominance
Lust Plague
Steel Dominance
Others
31 Flavors of Kink
Three Days of Dominance
Rough Surrender
Blood Glyphs
Cataclysm Blues (a free erotic post apocalyptic novella)
Needle Rain (epic fantasy – not erotic)

39646419R00115

Made in the USA
San Bernardino, CA
01 October 2016